Mrs. Darling
Librarian

Coach Ostraticki
Physical Education

Mrs. Harrington
English

Mrs. Gage
Lunchroom Monitor

ZACK DELACRUZ

UPSTAGED

ZACK DELACRUZ

UPSTAGED

By Jeff Anderson

STERLING CHILDREN'S BOOKS

New York

STERLING CHILDREN'S BOOKS
New York

An Imprint of Sterling Publishing
1166 Avenue of the Americas
New York, NY 10036

ISBN 978-1-4549-3115-7

Distributed in Canada by Sterling Publishing Co., Inc.
c/o Canadian Manda Group, 664 Annette Street
Toronto, Ontario M6S 2C8, Canada
Distributed in the United Kingdom by GMC Distribution Services
Castle Place, 166 High Street, Lewes, East Sussex BN7 1XU, England
Distributed in Australia by NewSouth Books
45 Beach Street, Coogee, NSW 2034, Australia

For information about custom editions, special sales, and premium and corporate purchases, please contact Sterling Special Sales at 800-805-5489 or specialsales@sterlingpublishing.com.

Manufactured in the United States of America

Lot #:
2 4 6 8 10 9 7 5 3 1
09/18

sterlingpublishing.com

Illustrations and design by Andrea Miller

No space of regret can make amends for one life's opportunity misused.

—**Charles Dickens**, *A Christmas Carol*

CONTENTS

I've never figured out why laughing gets you into trouble, but it *does*.

Adults spend tons of time worried kids aren't happy enough, but when you do have some fun, it's always at the wrong time. Here's some advice:

Just zip it.

Don't laugh.

Don't enjoy yourself.

Don't say a word.

Or the next thing you know, you'll end up like me, doing something you don't want to do.

Mrs. Harrington's English class was supposed to be browsing for books in the library. I stood by a bank of bookshelves with the usual suspects: Marquis, my best friend; Cliché, who was still crushing hard on Marquis;

and the indefinable, original Janie. We weren't exactly browsing *for* books as much as *in* one—our favorite: *The Enormous Book of World Records.*

"*Híjole!* Wow!" Janie held open to the book's spread on the world's smallest woman. In the blurry photo, a doll-sized lady stood on a small footstool.

"Wha'?" Cliché blurted. "It says here, she wears doll clothes from the American Girl shop."

"And she's twenty-three years old!" Janie nodded, skimming the entry.

"Man, that *is* old. I bet she's got a lot of American Girl reward points by now!" Cliché added, fascinated.

But I wasn't paying much attention to the smallest lady in the world. She didn't fascinate me like Abhi did. Abhi was not the smallest, but since the day she arrived a few weeks earlier, she was the most interesting girl at Davy Crockett Middle School. After checking out a Nancy Drew novel, she lounged at a table on the other side of the library, reading.

She crossed her red Keds and slid them back under her chair, her toes pointing down like a ballerina. Even though we were friends, Abhi was still—like the book in her hands—a mystery. I couldn't joke around or hang out with her the way I did with Marquis, Janie, and Cliché. I guess because José always gets to her first, or at least gets her attention. I wonder how I could be more attention-getting.

"Hey, Zack, do you think this lady could ride a Chihuahua like a horse?" Marquis elbowed me.

Cliché and Janie cackled loudly, and Cliché yelled,

"You didn't just say that, Marquis!"

Hands on his hips, Marquis posed like a superhero. "I am Humor Man!"

Shhh! I tried to stop the disruption before Mrs. Darling—the world's loudest, most energetic, and most involved librarian—put us in charge of shelving books or running another school fundraiser, or something worse.

But my *shhhh* was too late. My friends and I were going down like dominoes. And on my watch! Were we going to get sent to the office? We'd already been warned once today.

"Well, well, well." Mrs. Darling rested her rose-smelling hands on Marquis's and my shoulders. Using her green eyes like lasers, she targeted each of us. I couldn't tell if we were in trouble or if we would get away with it. We all grinned at once, trying to put on the charm.

"We sure do enjoy library time, Mrs. Darling." Marquis smiled up at her, batting his long eyelashes. Cliché snorted at his obvious insincerity. Then the giggles bubbled up, and the more we tried to hold the snickers in, the funnier it got. Even though we knew we should stop, we couldn't. Somehow knowing we *shouldn't* laugh made us laugh even harder. Dad calls it *church giggles*. Cliché hiccupped, Marquis snorted, and Janie sprayed spit as her cackle cut loose, causing the four of us to burst into even louder uncontrollable laughter.

"Yes." Janie tried to save us. "Books are entertainment, like the movies, Mrs. Darling."

"You and your friends like entertainment a lot, it appears." Mrs. Darling crossed her arms.

We stopped laughing.

Was that a question? I wondered. I wasn't sure what the right answer was. It felt like a trick. By the silence, I don't think anyone else knew either.

"You like entertainment, and it's obvious you already know the art of *vocal projection*, as evidenced by your outbursts today." She pulled us in even tighter, so tight it was uncomfortable. "I have just the opportunity for you all to utilize your talents to their fullest."

Opportunity was one of those words adults use when they want you to do something hard. What was she going to drop on us now?

"**W**hat do you mean by *projection*?" Cliché asked, hand on her hip.

"Great question, Cliché." Mrs. Darling pressed her hand on an oversized cheetah-print scarf, which swooped around her neck like a medieval shield. "As in, the art of being *heard*." She widened her stance and performed to the entire library. "As in the *thea-TUH*!" She thrust her arms up toward the ceiling tiles. Making eye contact with her audience around the library, she thumped her chest and extended her right arm outward. "As in, projecting one's voice to the back of the *thea-TUH*!"

The class flinched at the sheer volume.

"Why is she yelling?" Cliché whispered.

"I don't know," Marquis said, shrugging and sticking his fingers in his ears. "Maybe she's mad."

5

"She's not mad," Janie assured us. "She's talking about the smell of the grea*sss*epaint and the roar of the crowd." People used to tease Janie about her lisp, but now they just see it as a part of her, like her brown hair. Janie handed the book off to Cliché and joined in Mrs. Darling's show. "She's *projecting* so the audience can hear every *ss*crumptious*sss* word of the playwright!"

It sounded like Janie was now an expert on movies *and* the theater.

"Sorry Mrs. D., and no disrespect, Janie," Cliché scoffed, "but we're not interested in the *thea-TAH*, with its smells and greases and whatnots." She turned back to *The Enormous Book of World Records,* which she now controlled.

"Ma says I have a dramatic flair." Marquis stood straighter, smiling.

Thud!

Cliché dropped the huge record book to the floor.

"Oh, Marquis!" Mrs. Darling cupped his face in her hands. "You are just the kind of man I hope will show up at the auditions tomorrow."

"Did I hear someone is interested in . . . a *man*?" El Pollo Loco, José's alter ego, interrupted, stroking his imaginary mustache.

Everybody watched.

"There is no need for, how you say, *an audition*." He gently took Mrs. Darling's hand. She attempted to pull it away, but José gripped it tighter and stared straight into her green eyes. "I am *the* man you are looking for, I can assure you, my lovely library lady." I thought he might

6

bend down and kiss her hand, right on her old library-green fingernail polish.

"She's telling us about the *theater*, El." Janie nudged herself between Mrs. Darling and José. He stepped back as if Janie were radioactive, releasing Mrs. Darling's hand.

"It's about *acting*—not about who you *are*." Janie thumped her chest as Mrs. Darling had. "Theater is about who you *could* be." She may not have been radioactive, but something had infected Janie, and it was the acting bug.

"Not being yourself? That could be a good role for you, Janie," José jabbed, flipping up the red collar on his uniform shirt. *"Ha! HA!"* When no one laughed, he put his collar back down. Disappointed, José added, "Justkidding."

For the last couple of weeks, after multiple detentions, whenever José insulted or pranked anyone, he immediately added a quick *justkidding* at the end, all at once, as if it were one word, and as if it were an eraser that made his harsh words disappear into little dark rolls of nothing. He was changing a little, I guess. "Awareness is the first step," the school counselor, Dr. Smith-Cortez always said. At least José was trying to erase his mean jokes, but even so, his victims were still left hurt.

"Acting is a way to entertain people *without* hurting feelings." Mrs. Darling mussed José's hair.

"Hey, Miss Library Lady, don't touch my *do*!" El Pollo Loco raised his hand to protect his part.

Ignoring him, Mrs. Darling picked up a large gold bell and raised it above her head. José ducked. *"Hear ye! Hear ye! Hear ye!"* Mrs. Darling rang the bell, like the town criers we learned about in fifth-grade American history. "For the fifteenth year in a row, as sponsor, director, and playwright, I'm happy to announce the Actin' Alamos' annual production of Charles Dickens's *A Christmas Carol*."

"My nana's name is Carol!" Chewy Johnson said as he joined the growing group.

Mrs. Darling slammed the bell on a shelf, sighing, "Be that as it may, I am searching for people who can project for onstage roles."

Not me, I thought, trying not to make eye contact with Mrs. Darling. I wouldn't want an onstage role to save my life. I know how this works: I get volunteered to do something I don't want to do. Can't do. And then I'm supposed to pull myself up by my bootstraps, and I don't even know what bootstraps are. I don't even own a pair of boots. I definitely needed to stay away from this. I tried to step away. I could hear my heart thumping, and it wasn't a good kind of excitement. My survival instinct was kicking in, like Mr. Stankowitz taught us about. I was choosing flight instead of fight.

"What about backstage roles?" Bossy Blythe Balboa asked. Now that Blythe was taking the focus, I felt relieved and was able to slip back a few steps. Blythe continued, "I want to be in charge of stuff." Her eyes widened. Besides being the sixth grade's student council representative, she was always trying to be in charge of stuff like cooperative groups. In her eyes, cooperative groups were created so that everyone would cooperate with whatever she decided.

"There will be both onstage and offstage roles." Mrs.

Darling tried to keep moving forward, but the questions flew at her, splatting on her surprised face like bugs on the windshield of Mom's Honda.

"What do you mean *roles*?" Cliché asked.

"It's like a part in the play, like a starring role." Janie's eyes glazed over and her shoulders rolled back.

I took a few more steps back and leaned on a bookshelf. Count me out. I wasn't going to star in anything. I turned toward the nonfiction shelf and pretended to browse.

"I have more of an *on*stage look, don't I?" El smoothed his black hair.

Now even I shortened José's nickname to El. Only a few months ago, he was the school bully. Now he was looking for other ways to get all the attention—especially from Abhi. So I guess now he's the type that goes out for parts in plays, performing for everybody. Not me. Not ever.

"How much does this theater gig pay?" El asked, squinting.

"We'll all be paid through the adoration and applause of an appreciative audience, like on those singing competition shows you watch." The class gathered closer to Mrs. Darling, leaning in.

"Is *A Christmas Carol* that movie with that goofy kid Ralphie with glasses?" Marquis asked, zipping his powder-blue warm-up jacket up and down.

"Yeah, I love that movie," I nodded, stepping toward the group again, "that blond kid keeps wanting a Red Ryder air rifle the whole time."

The class laughed and nodded.

"A goofy kid with glasses?" El zoomed in on me like an airborne drone. "Well, well, well, Zack." Target identified. "That sounds like it was written just for you."

Embarrassment missile deployed.

Not *justkidding*.

"**N**o!" Janie shook her head. "Absolutely not! *You're* talking about the classic holiday-time feel-good film, *A Christmas STORY*, nineteen eighty-three, starring a bespectacled Peter Billingsley," Janie, the movie *and play* expert, explained. "*A Christmas CAROL* has been made into multiple movies and TV specials far too numerous to name. But I can say this with certainty: *A Christmas CAROL* is far, far older and more dramatic than *A Christmas STORY*. In fact, in twenty seventeen *A Christmas Story* was performed live on TV."

That's right, Janie. Keep talking, I thought. Everyone would forget all about El's humiliating drone attack on me.

"You mean like *old* from when Mrs. Library Lady was a kid?" José popped his head toward Mrs. Darling.

"I guess," Janie squinted, trying to do the mental math.

For a few seconds, everyone looked Mrs. Darling up and down, from her swooped-up-like-a-tropical-storm red hair to her lime-green jumpsuit, ready for space travel. Her fingerlike toes struggled to free themselves from their gold sandal prisons. The finger-toes looked like tentacles, with their painted orange heads reaching for the library carpet, undulating like the pink squid in the science video we saw in Mr. Stankowitz's class.

"*Wooow!*" the shocked class sighed. Nobody could wrap their heads around a time so ancient as when Mrs. Darling was a kid.

Abhi walked up, all smiles. "*A Christmas CAROL* is the play about a cheapskate named Ebenezer Scrooge."

Finally! When Abhi talked, I listened. I loved the way she said the character's name: *Ebenezer Scrooge.* It sounded poetic, like when she said my name, too: *Zack Delacroooz.*

Blythe barged in between Abhi and me, holding a blue notepad like a reporter in an old-timey movie. "When did you say the auditions were again, huh?"

"I didn't." Mrs. Darling cleared her throat. "But so glad you asked, Blythe. Auditions—tryouts for the play— are tomorrow after school." Mrs. Darling glided toward the bulletin board with a red sheet of paper.

The class rushed behind her to see what the sheet said. Mrs. Darling stuck white and green pushpins into each corner.

Blythe shoved her way to the front and began reading

the bulletin aloud, even though nobody had asked her to—or wanted her to.

AUDITIONS FOR
The Davy Crockett Actin' Alamos'
Annual Production of

A CHRISTMAS CAROL
By Charles Dickens
November 12th

After School in the Cafetorium
Adapted, Produced, and Directed by
Judith K. Darling, MIS

Blythe stood so close behind Mrs. Darling that she was unable to step away from the sign. "What do you need me to be in charge of? I'm student council representative for sixth grade, so of course you want me to do something that requires upper management skills." In her white cardigan, Blythe looked like a life-size pushpin, pinning Mrs. Darling to the bulletin board.

Mrs. Darling struggled to free herself. Wiggling herself free, she grunted, "So very helpful." But it didn't sound like she thought it was helpful at all.

"I used to fancy myself an actress in my day." Mrs. Harrington, our English teacher, pulled her hair behind her ears, stepping away from her guard post at the checkout desk. "If it helps, I'll give extra credit to anyone who works on the play."

"Wonderful idea, Mrs. Harrington," Mrs. Darling said, breathing easier now that she wasn't pinned to the bulletin board like an announcement. "Every little bit helps. *Huzzah!* Team library and language arts unite!"

"Seriously?" José walked up to Mrs. Harrington. "Because I need whole lot of points for not turning in my at-home reading log."

"I turn in *two* reading logs every week, don't I, Mrs. Harrington?" Blythe announced, eyeing Mrs. Darling so the woman could see what she was missing.

"Yes, you do," Mrs. Harrington answered. "I always enjoy having *extra* papers to grade." But it didn't sound like she meant it.

Extra credit changed everything for sixth-graders. Even I was curious now. Extra credit was the cherry on top of the play audition sundae. In middle school, teachers only need say two words, *extra credit,* and students are in the palm of their hands. Kids will do more for extra credit than for any other kind of credit.

"Do you still get credit if you stay backstage?" Blythe asked.

"Of course, dear," Mrs. Darling replied.

Maybe I *could* take on a behind-the-scenes role. Maybe I *could* raise and lower the curtain. I mean: *extra credit.* Who could resist that? And maybe I could spend some friend time with Abhi after school.

"I'll do the makeup for the play," Sophia said, pursing her lips at herself in a compact mirror. "But only if I don't

14

have to go to all the rehearsals." She looked around the class, explaining to us with her wise, second-time-in-sixth-grade voice, "my boyfriend, Raymond, and I usually have tardy detention after school."

"Well . . ." Mrs. Darling knelt down to retrieve *The Enormous Book of World Records* from the floor. "I suppose so."

Everybody really could have a role, it seemed.

"I still get my extra credit though, right?" Sophia peered over her mirror at Mrs. Harrington. I bet Sophia could be in *The Enormous Book of World Records* for least possible effort ever.

Mrs. Harrington glanced at Mrs. Darling. They both shrugged.

"I suppose so." Mrs. Harrington and Mrs. Darling shared a look.

"Then I'm in." Sophia snapped her compact closed and dropped it in her purse.

Then Mrs. D. slid the record book to its proper place on the shelf.

"Hey, what do you think, Zack?" Marquis asked. "Are you going to audition for the play or what?"

"Me?" I said, shaking my head. "No way!"

"Oh, come on, it'll be fun," Marquis added.

"Yeah," said Cliché.

"That settles it," Janie added. "*We're* doing it."

"So, Mrs. Darling, this whole *you*-being-the-director thing," Blythe asked, "Is that like a done deal? Or—"

"For the love of Pete!" Mrs. Darling took in deep breath. "Yes, Blythe, it's a very done deal. I will be directing the show."

"How about assistant director?" Blythe suggested, putting her finger up to her lip. This girl never gets the hint. For sixth-grade representative, you'd think she would have people skills other than telling them what to do.

Mrs. Darling's eyes quickly scanned the class, searching for anyone other than Blythe.

Her eyes landed on Chewy first, because he was lumbering toward her. "After careful consideration of all candidates, I've chosen Chewy . . ." Mrs. Darling leaned in and whispered, "What's your last name, dear?"

"Johnson?" Chewy looked surprised.

"Yes, Chewy Johnson will be the Actin' Alamos' assistant director. The first role is filled."

"But I just wanted to go to the bathroom," Chewy said.

"But . . . but, but . . ." Blythe sputtered.

"If *if*s and *but*s were candy and nuts, we'd all have a merry Christmas." A smile spread across Mrs. Darling's face. I think she was cracking herself up. At least grown-ups get to have a good time.

Blythe closed her notebook, swung around, and pouted at Fiction A–D, whispering something.

"Zack, are you going to try out for the part of Ebenezer Scrooge?" Abhi stood beside me again. "He's the most important role in the play. I think you'd be great at it."

"Yeah, Zack," Janie said.

There Abhi was, saying my name again. A fragrance followed her everywhere she went, a fragrance as sweet as the spring breeze car freshener that hung from the air vent of Mom's Honda.

Until that moment, I wasn't even sure I wanted an onstage role, no matter what my friends said or did. And I still wasn't. But now Abhi wanted me to play this Ebenezer Scrooge guy. I felt wanted—which was weird. But it felt good.

I don't know if it was the way she stood right next to me, the way she said *Ebenezer Scrooge*, or the way her hair smelled like a spring breeze, but suddenly I was swept up in the moment. I was that guy who might say yes to life. In that one moment, I could be the kind of guy who auditioned for plays. I was about to spit out the impossible words, "Yes, I'll try out for Ebenezer Scrooge." But then I started thinking of all the trouble saying yes could get you into. Like the time I was in charge of the candy sale with El Pollo Loco, which led to the car wash, and then the dance. Or all the ways I messed up the last time I tried to spend more time with Abhi: ripped pants, choo choo *chones*, the dodgeball assassin incident. Once the snowball rolls, it picks up more snow whether you want it to or not, getting bigger and bigger.

Before I uttered a word, El Pollo Loco squeezed between Abhi and me.

CHAPTER 4

ALL SHE COULD MANAGE

"**A**bhi, I think I have figured out who should be that *Had-a-Tweezer* Scrooge guy," José announced, flashing his grin.

"*Eh-BA-NEEZ-er*, El!" Abhi turned her sparkling smile toward El Pollo Loco.

Great! Here was my chance to be the attention-getter, and José was, once again, stealing my thunder.

"That's great news!" Abhi patted José on the back, "I hoped somebody good would go for the lead role. Plays are so much fun!"

Abhi! He didn't even know the main character's name. I didn't either exactly, but why him? Why not me? My stomach lurched. I wanted to yell, *Wait! Look at me, Abhi! I am somebody good, and I'm going to try out for Scrooge.* But I didn't. I just stood there, letting José soak up all my attention.

"Yeah, I'm a great actor." José nodded his head up and down, slower than slow, like a real creep. "My mom always believes whatever I tell her."

If I were more like El, I'd probably say, *Hey, over here, Abs! Remember me? You were just asking me if was auditioning for Scrooge, and I was about to say yes.* But I'm not like José. I'm like me, keeping my trap shut, letting everything go the way it goes.

José just took whatever he wanted. I've never been like that.

My courage slid through my fingers like fine store-bought sand, pouring onto the library floor. Why would I even consider trying out for Scrooge anyway? I guess I could take a backstage role. That's where I belonged anyway. But what was the point? I could never compete with José, the attention-getter crazy chicken.

"I think I might like to go out for the role of Scrooge as well," Marquis announced.

What?

Somebody pull the emergency brake on the bus! My head involuntarily popped toward my best friend, causing some kind of friendship whiplash. *Now Marquis wanted to be Scrooge, too?* This couldn't be happening. Was this some kind of nightmare where everyone had the guts to take an onstage part except me? Wake me up! Mom? Dad? Somebody? Please!

"Oh, this is simply splendid news, thespians." Mrs. Darling beamed.

"What'd you call me?" José squinted.

In a British accent, Janie explained, "A *thespian* is

someone who participates in the *thea-TUH*!" Janie seemed to know a lot about this *thea-TUH* thing. She even knew how to say it. And speak British. Man, there was so much I didn't know. So much I'd probably never know.

"Why are you talking British, Janie?" El asked.

"Duh," Cliché said, bobbing her head. "That's how you can tell she's *acting.*"

Janie curtsied.

Once Marquis piled on that he was trying out for Scrooge too, it felt like globs of dry organic peanut butter clogged my throat. My mouth opened, but nothing came out.

"That's so funny you're trying out for Scrooge, Marquis." Cliché touched his arm. "I was just getting ready to say that *I* was auditioning for *Mrs.* Scrooge." Cliché too? Was there a plot against me?

"There is no *Mrs.* Scrooge, silly," Abhi giggled, explaining to Cliché. "But there is a Mrs. Cratchit."

Cliché rolled her eyes.

"Who else is in?" Abhi put her hand out flat in the center of those who'd gathered around Mrs. Darling. Abhi, the new quarterback for the Actin' Alamos, brought us in like we were her team. Team Abhi.

Without a word, I smacked my hand on top of Abhi's before anyone else knew what had happened. Starting now, I'd said to myself, I would be the guy who acted first and thought later.

Scowling, José slapped his hand down on mine—hard. Janie's hand followed, then Marquis's, then Cliché placed her hand on Marquis's. They both giggled. We looked around to see who else was going to bring it in for the Actin' Alamos. And I wondered what I thought I was doing.

"I just lotioned my hands." Sophia held up her shimmering hands, like a surgeon on TV. "Soooo . . ." She scrunched up her nose and stared down at our pile of hands like they were riddled with some contagious skin disease.

Chewy paced back and forth, and then his hand hung above the stack of hands.

"What happens if you have to go to the bathroom during the play?" Chewy looked pleadingly over his shoulder at Mrs. Darling.

"You won't be onstage. You're my assistant director." Mrs. Darling said. "You can go whenever you feel the urge."

"Hurray!" Chewy disappeared.

"*Urine* the play," El called after him. "*Justkidding.*"

Blythe cleared her throat. "I know you already said who you'd chosen for assistant director, but don't you think you should consider *moi*: Blythe Balboa, student council representative?" She handed Mrs. Darling a business card, which she'd scribbled on a torn-out page of her notebook. "I'm more assistant director material? I mean . . ." She looked over her shoulder to the door Chewy had escaped through and shrugged. Man, this girl is a sneaky snake.

"I see you more as a *stage manager*, Blythe." Mrs. Darling cut her off.

Blythe stopped talking. Her face went from mad to maleficent, like the Disney villain. "Hear that, y'all? I manage it *all*!" Blythe projected her voice to the entire library—and beyond—motioning her hands at the entirety of the universe. "Everything on the stage, I manage." She pointed to herself. "Two words and four syllables to remember: *Stage Man-a-ger.*" She shot two finger pistols in the air, blew off the imaginary smoke, and shoved her hands into her white cardigan pockets like holsters.

"Bossy Blythe has spoken," José added. "*Justkidding.*"

Everyone laughed this time, except Blythe. She gave José a dirty look and scribbled something in her little notebook, like she knew something we didn't.

L ater, in math class, while we were supposed to be subtracting integers, I laid my head down. Even though I knew I couldn't audition for Scrooge, I couldn't stop thinking about it either: I regretted not speaking up. How would my life have changed or turned out better if I *had* spoken up? And Marquis auditioning for Scrooge had gotten under my skin. He is supposed to be my best friend. I mean, sure, he didn't know I wanted the role. And I don't want it. But he always does things before me, like we're in a competition. And I was losing. Big-time.

"What are you doing?" Marquis whispered, interrupting my nap.

"I'm resting my eyes for a minute," I whispered back without lifting my head.

"Those math problems aren't going to answer themselves."

"And why not?" I yawned. "I think it's time for math to grow up and solve its own problems."

"Okay," Marquis snickered. "That was a good one."

And I knew it was. But what I didn't know was what to do next. My mind spun like a garbage disposal, breaking my thoughts into little bits that kept getting rinsed down the drain. I took a deep breath. Whenever I'm worried about school, Mom has always calmed me down by asking, "What are the facts as we know them?" I was desperate, so I tried it.

Fact 1: I wasn't trying out for Scrooge.

Fact 2: Part of me still wanted to audition for Scrooge.

The two facts argued with each other. Afraid to mess up or miss out, I felt like I was caught in one of those bamboo finger traps we had gotten in science a few weeks ago on Science Friday—the day science becomes fun with real-world experiments and thinking. Usually it's a dud, but this one was memorable.

wwmm

Each of us got our own finger trap, but Mr. Stankowitz called them *bamboo finger puzzles* instead, because he's a teacher. The finger puzzles were colorful bamboo strips woven into skinny tubes about the length of an empty toilet paper roll, but only as wide as your index finger.

Whatever you call them, they were cool, because they weren't even science at all. They were a magic trick! Once you stick your index fingers into both ends of the tube, you're trapped. And the puzzle begins. You try to pull your fingers free, but the more you pull, the tighter the tube becomes.

In class that day, Mr. Stankowitz had said, "That's traction. Does that help you solve the puzzle?"

We all struggled for a minute or two when suddenly Chewy leapt up from his seat, knocking his chair over. "Get me out of this thing!" He yanked his hands apart so hard that the tube got longer and thinner.

"Chewy, calm down," Mr. Stankowitz warned, stepping toward him. But he was too late. Chewy had ripped the finger puzzle to shreds.

"*Yoooouch!*" Chewy screamed, shaking both hands, running for the door. "I'm telling my mom!" He grabbed the bathroom pass, which was an actual toilet seat, the part you sit on. It's very embarrassing to carry a gross old toilet seat through the hallways, announcing that you're going to the bathroom, so nobody ever uses it. Except Chewy. The rest of us just went during passing period, if at all. That's a whole other story.

Mr. Stankowitz explained his reasoning on the first day of school, which immediately earned him the nickname Mr. Stanko-WIZ. Only someone who really had to go would carry that disgusting thing down the hall. And the way Chewy ripped apart his finger puzzle and slammed the door, carrying the toilet seat was the least of his worries.

Puzzled, we all looked at Mr. Stankowitz for our next move. None of us wanted to be a Chewy.

"There's an easier way than *that* to solve the puzzle." Mr. Stankowitz motioned his head at the door.

Seconds later, Marquis the Magician's tube dropped to his desk.

"So how'd you get your fingers free, Marquis?" Mr. Stankowitz asked, smiling.

"I don't know." Marquis smiled and shrugged. "It's like instead of pulling, I just gave up and pushed my fingers together and then they slid right out." Right after Marquis's revelation, finger traps began dropping on desks and bouncing on the floor. Everybody *ooh*ed and *ahh*ed.

"I already knew that," Blythe said, dropping her finger puzzle in the garbage can. But we all knew she hadn't.

✳✳✳✳

The finger trap of auditioning for the play had me pulling Fact 1 and Fact 2 away from each other. Maybe I just needed to relax and let the trap fall to the floor. I thought about it. If I kept pulling so hard, I might tear the trap—or the facts, or me—in half. I didn't want to be a Chewy. I wanted to solve my problem calmly and easily, like Marquis. You know, it's really hard when your best friend is always besting you. But I could be calm and logical like Marquis, so back to the facts.

Fact 3: Marquis and José had already said they were auditioning for Scrooge, and I hadn't said a word.

Outdone again. By José *and* Marquis. On that day, like every day, I had felt proud Marquis was my friend. But today, I thought he was kind of a know-it-all. Like he had to be first at everything, like he was competing with me. That day he was in my way, like José. Marquis and José

26

were yet another finger trap, forcing me to pull away from both sides.

Fact 4: Both of them had beaten me to the punch, announcing their plans before I had a chance to.

My mind yanked even harder at both ends of that audition finger puzzle. On one end, Abhi *wanted* me to audition for Ebenezer Scrooge, and I *wanted* to show her I could do it. But on the other end of the trap, I didn't know if I could. Plus José and Marquis were pulling at me too. It would look like I was just doing what they did. Still a follower. What do you do when all your fingers have bamboo traps on them?

If I audition for Ebenezer Scrooge against my best friend, is that pulling at the finger trap or pushing in?

"You better get working on those integers." Marquis pushed on my shoulder.

A know-it-all bossy betrayer.

Wait.

Marquis hadn't done anything. Plus I didn't even want the part. I half lifted my head up from my math book. Luckily, Mr. Gonzalez was busy grading our weekly assessments—too busy to notice what we were or weren't doing.

"Get started, Nap Delacruz!" Marquis warned, scratching down numbers.

"Five more minutes," I yawned, resting my head back down.

"The bell is ringing in five minutes!" Marquis said.

In my head, I told myself I could do whatever I wanted. Marquis was not the boss of me. But would he be mad if I went out for Scrooge too? I was afraid of so many things—even Marquis. Instead of talking to him about what was going on, I was sneaking naps and daydreaming about finger traps. I was still a little afraid of everything and everyone. But Mom reminded me the other day that most of the stuff I worried about never happened. Worrying was kind of like a finger trap—pulling at it only made things worse.

Marquis poked me again with the eraser end of his trusty mechanical pencil.

I sat up, and my squinting eyes landed on one of Mr. Gonzalez's laminated motivational posters:

> You have to be ODD to be number one.
>
> —Anonymous

This motivational message seemed to be from a poster god named Anonymous. Have you ever noticed how many quotes are from this Anonymous person? Or Albert Einstein? There were a lot of those, too.

Anyway, maybe I *could* decide what to do. I mean, the letter *I* kind of looked like the numeral one. Maybe trying out for the lead role would be an *odd* thing for me to do. So maybe I just needed to do the opposite of what I want to do, so I could see what number one feels like.

The little voice in my head, which was sometimes my friend and sometimes my foe, taunted me. *What makes you think you can do this?*

"Well, evil foe, so far this year, I've rescued the school

chocolate bar sale, helped get sixth grade into the dance, and saved Abhi from a runaway train. So . . ."

"Who are you talking to, Zack?" Marquis asked.

"Nobody." I hadn't realized I'd said that out loud. However, talking to yourself is definitely odd, so I guessed I was on the right track.

So? The foe voice in my head answered.

I gazed at the slobber spot on problem 46. Mr. G. wouldn't like that. But Mr. G. would be happy I had problem-solved the entire period. And I came up with four ways to solve the problem.

1. Take the easy way as usual and go with whatever backstage role Mrs. Darling assigns me.

2. Or, I could do the *odd* thing and try out for Ebenezer Scrooge, and maybe have a chance to be number 1 (Number Poster Wisdom).

3. Or, I could end up looking like a stupid fool no matter what I did, so what have I got to lose?

4. Ask a friend for advice.

I started thinking about who I would become, not who I'd been. And the next odd thing that popped in my head was: *Ask Abhi for advice.* I figured once I did that, I'd know what to do about the audition.

It just so happens this was a week I was at Mom's and took the bus with Abhi. What are the odds of that, huh? That's right, Mr. G. I used math in a real-world situation.

After school, more rested, I swaggered up the bus steps. My nap had helped, and so had the motivational poster. The bus ride would be the perfect place to ask Abhi about the play and what I should do. Maybe once I found out more about the play, I'd know if trying out for Scrooge was the right choice.

In other news, I'd finally become a master at switching buses every week—one week at Dad's, one week at Mom's. It felt normal now. My normal. Since it was my week to live at Mom's, there'd be no Marquis to sit next to on the bus, to talk with or calm me down. The weird part was I felt okay about it. Now every odd thing lit my path to numero uno.

As I strolled to the middle of the bus, I imagined Abhi playing the new role of bus friend. I'd casually strike up a conversation about the play. After I saved Abhi from the train at the fiesta-val, we mostly just nodded and smiled at each other—no real conversations. But today I had questions, and Abhi had answers.

The seat next to her was empty.

I gulped. It was go time. My pits trickled a little stream down the inside of my red uniform shirt. I wondered if anyone could see it. Boy, was I glad Mom convinced me to start wearing deodorant.

"Hey." I faced Abhi.

"Hey, yourself," Abhi said, beaming.

"I was wondering if we could talk about the play." I cleared my throat. "It sounds like you know a lot about it."

"We did the play in Minnesota last year," Abhi nodded. She tapped the vinyl beside her. "Hurry up and sit down before that Bossy Blythe nudges her way into this seat."

OMG. I forgot to breathe for a minute and just stood there. Abhi ASKED ME to sit down. Next to her. Doing the odd thing was all right. Usually I'd end up on a ripped-up bus seat with the foam cushion poking through. But next to Abhi, I got smooth forest-green vinyl. And she'd invited *me* to sit with her. Obvs, I was working it all—Smooth Moves Delacruz. That is, until I opened my mouth.

"Yeah, bossy is Blythe," I stumbled over my words. Not odd.

"Funny is Zack," Abhi teased. Being teased—not odd.

"Smart is Abhi." I tossed my head back, laughing. That *was* odd. Not worrying *was* odd. Good save I did. I was officially rocking odd. This would be our thing. We'd

Yoda all our sentences. See that? Me and Abhi had a thing, and I had just sat down. Thrilled I was.

"YoDA man!" Abhi shot back.

She gets me, I thought. "YoDA *Wo*-man!" I was playing the role of the guy who talks to anyone he wants—even girls. I wasn't slumping against the bus window trying to disappear anymore.

We snickered. Our eyes met for a moment, and she stopped laughing, and so I did. Uh oh, things were about to get real, I thought.

"ATTENTION, ATTENTION!" Blythe interrupted, standing in the bus aisle, a human bullhorn in a white cardigan. "As many of you are aware, I, Blythe Balboa, am *in charge* of the Actin' Alamos Annual Production of *A Christmas Carol*."

"And," Chewy interrupted, holding up his finger, "It's not the one about the blond kid with glasses who wants a BB gun."

"Hey, Chewy," Blythe stomped toward him. "You know what I appreciate about you interrupting me?" She leaned in, an inch from Chewy's face. "Jack SQUAT!"

Chewy flinched and mouthed *Sorry.* Then he slumped deep into his seat, clutching his orange backpack to his belly. Man, Blythe's as mean as a scraped knee.

"First rule of Drama Club," Blythe continued, walking up and down the aisle. "When I talk, everybody listens."

"Blythe, sit down!" Ms. Nancy, the bus driver, turned back, still gripping the steering wheel. Her voice was graveled from years of yelling "Sit down!"

"Oh," Blythe explained, "I'm pretty sure the stage

manager has special abilities to *not* follow the same rules as everyone else, so you go on ahead, Ms. Nancy. I *got* this." Blythe waved Ms. Nancy off and continued repeating what Mrs. Darling had already explained, but louder and more obnoxiously. "If you're auditioning tomorrow, you need a note from your parents saying it's okay for you to take the late bus home."

Static crackled. Ms. Nancy had switched on her intercom to compete with Bullhorn Blythe. "Blythe, I'm not moving this bus one inch until your bottom is in a seat." Ms. Nancy sounded like she needed a vacation. "Should I call Principal Akins over?"

"*Pshaw!* Don't be silly, Ms. Nancy." Blythe held her hands up like she had done nothing wrong. She sank into her seat.

"Over and out." Nancy switched off the intercom and started the bus.

Blythe cupped her hand to the right. "I guess Scrooge isn't the only one who's a grumpity grump, huh?" Blythe high-fived the girl next to her, but she just stared back silently, like the rest of us.

The bus rolled out of the parking lot with a bump, and Blythe kept her seat and kept talking. "Auditions will be tomorrow, Friday, at 3:00 p.m. sharp."

I tried to say something to Abhi whenever I thought Blythe was winding down.

"Wha—" I couldn't even get out the first word before Blythe blabbed again.

"Absolutely no one will be admitted after 3:01 p.m."

I tried again. "So what should I know about Scr—?

"The rules are really for *your* benefit," Blythe interrupted, "not mine."

I sighed. "I just want to know a few things—"

"As stage manager I'm just"—Blythe made air quotes—"'the enforcer.'" She wasn't only bossy: she'd taken it to a whole other level.

But you could say this about Blythe: She did what she wanted and didn't seem to care what other people thought. Oh, no: *I was not wishing to be more like Blythe? Was I?*

Or was I? That would, in fact, be odd. This was *odd*hausting.

I slumped into my seat—hopeless.

"Simmer down, Blythe!" Ms. Nancy shouted as she paused at a stop sign. "I'll turn this bus around and hand you off to Mr. Akins, if that's what you want." And we all knew from the sound of her voice, she would.

Blythe bowed her head and buttoned her lip.

"Now, Zack." Abhi looked toward me. "What did you want to talk about?"

Abhi just asked *me* a question about ME? Now that a space had opened for us to chat, I froze like a cherry Popsicle—and probably turned just as red.

"Zack?"

I couldn't blow this. I *wouldn't* blow this. "I've been thinking about trying out for the play."

"That's great!" Abhi said.

"But I . . . I . . ." Talking to someone as beautiful as Abhi sounds easy, but you have to remember to breathe.

"—But you're kind of nervous." She finished my sentence just the way I would've—If I could've.

34

I sighed out a big breath and turned toward her. "Exactly!" *Look who's talking now*, I thought. "How'd you know?" *Hey! Now I'm asking questions.* I pumped myself up.

"It's completely normal to be nervous about auditions, Zack. I know I am." She nodded.

Hear that? I'm normal and I'm like Abhi.

"Have you ever done a play before?" Abhi asked.

"Nope." I shook my head.

"Then it makes sense to be nervous." Abhi's gray eyes widened. "New things make me worry all the time. When it was my first day at Davy Crockett Middle School, you were one of the people who made me feel more comfortable."

"Really?"

"Yes, of course!" Abhi smiled. "Why would I say it if I didn't think it?"

She had a point.

"And I'll do the same for you at auditions tomorrow."

"You'll make me smile," I said.

"Yes, Zack. Just like you are now."

I threw my hands over my mouth. *Smooth move, Delacruz.*

Abhi laughed.

And I joined her.

CHAPTER 7
SNACK DELACRUZ

After I climbed off the bus, I waved to Abhi, who stuck her face through an open window, smiling. As the bus ground to a start, I watched Abhi, and then the bus, till it turned a corner.

How do you like me now? I strutted up the sidewalk to the door. I had realized something. Doing new stuff can turn out cool, but sometimes it won't. This is how we discover what we like. We try new things and we don't know what will happen. That's living on the edge.

When I unlocked Mom's door, I hung my backpack on the hook that has a gold Z above it. It's not real gold, but I pretend it is. I shuffled into the kitchen to scrounge for a snack. *How about that?* I was chatting with Abhi like a boss. I didn't know I had it in me. I slipped off my shoes without untying them. For a second, I thought about putting them

36

where they belonged. But I felt free.

"Everything has its place," Mom always said.

But I'd had a big day, so I left them on the kitchen floor, like I owned the place. Skating on my socks, I slid across the cool tile to the refrigerator. Once I opened it, the light and familiar hum calmed me.

Mom's house was big and empty. It was lonely and quiet before I turned on the TV. At the Villa De La Fountaine, where Dad lives, a commotion always erupts from the apartment above, beside, or under. So, at Mom's, while I was alone in her gigantic quiet kitchen, I entertained myself by narrating every move I made, like a pro-wrestling announcer on TV.

"Ladies and gentlemen, appliances of all ages, today's snacks will be eaten by the king of the *Snack Down*, none other than"—I reverberated my voice—"Snack DelaCRU-U-U-UZ!" My audience of cabinets and stainless-steel appliances watched in hushed amazement.

When I did stuff like that, Mom said I was a ham. I wondered if tomorrow at auditions I'd show off. Could my whole *Snack Down* show have been preparing me for this play all this time? This part? This moment? I had never really thought of myself as an actor, but maybe I'd always been one. "He's taking the peanut butter and tortillas from the pantry. Can he balance them without falling on his face or fumbling the food to the floor? Yes! Ladies and gentlemen, his skills are unmatched in the world of snack management.

"In the ring with Snack today is the pummeling PBJ Roll-Up!" I tossed the whole-wheat tortilla on a paper towel. "The tortilla is down on the mat. What will Snack do?" I opened the drawer and grabbed a knife. In a loud whisper, I continued, "Folks, he's spreading the organic peanut butter he bought at Wholesome Foods with his mother!

"But wait, he's not through with that tortilla yet, folks. Oh, no, he's smearing apricot jelly all over the peanut butter!" I rolled the tortilla up tight. "He's finishing his opponent off with a classic tight roll. The crowd goes wild. Snack Delacruz wins with the old PBJ Roll-Up."

I poured a glass of almond milk. "*Snack Down* was brought to you by our sponsor, almond milk—a cool and silky addition to any snack." With a full mouth, I left the kitchen with, "Good afternoon, everybody, see you next time."

I strolled to the couch, plopped down, and pressed the TV remote to turn on *Judge Joe's Court*. During the commercials, I stared at the phone, wondering if I should call Marquis. But what would I say? I guess I could talk about sitting next to Abhi. What would *he* say about me thinking about trying out for Scrooge? Would he encourage me? Would I encourage him? Plus, why wasn't he calling me? Why do I have to be the one who calls? As a commercial for anxiety medication finished listing all side effects, I decided it would be odd to *not* call Marquis. Though it would be odd to call Janie. I didn't know if I was taking this odd thing too far.

A knot tightened in the pit of my stomach. Or maybe it was a ball of whole wheat tortilla and organic peanut butter. I wondered if the knot in my stomach was an example of *internal conflict* like Mrs. Harrington had talked about in English last week: *Man vs. Self.* More like *Boy vs. Stomach* or *Friend vs. Friend.* There's no shortage of conflict in middle school.

I sucked in a deep breath.

The poster image from math class rolled across my brain: "To be number one, you have to be ODD." One thing was for sure. I felt odd. It was odd to *not* call Marquis. If only I had my own phone, I could text him. But I don't. And neither does he. So that was an odd thing to think. It was also odd that I walked up to Abhi and sat with her on the bus, and it's odd we talked and hung out and smiled and laughed. It's odd that Mom's cabinets and appliances are the biggest audience I've ever performed for so far. And I realized the oddest thing of all was that I didn't want to play the shy and lonely role after school anymore.

I was going to try out for Ebenezer Scrooge.

By the next day at breakfast, I wanted to be Ebenezer Scrooge so much I could taste it in my blueberry Pop-Tart. To be ready to audition, I had until 3 p.m. to find out as much as I could about the play. When I know more about things, I feel more confident.

The weird thing was, I still had told only one person that I was auditioning—Abhi.

I hadn't really said anything to anyone else.

Not Janie.

Not Cliché.

Not even Marquis.

Part of the problem was that I didn't know *what* to say—or *how* to say it—and the longer I waited, the harder it was to carry this knowledge, like some kind of backpack overstuffed with textbooks.

How did all this auditioning stuff work anyway? Are you required to say what part you're auditioning for? Had Marquis and El already called it, like calling shotgun for the front seat of a car? All I knew was I was tired of taking the backseat. I wanted to be like Mr. Gonzalez's poster with its orange number one, with its curly white letters of encouragement. No more backseat for me. The backseat was normal, and I wanted to be odd.

"So what role are you going to try out for?" Marquis asked.

Silently, I licked my finger and dabbed up Pop-Tart crumbs off my Styrofoam breakfast tray. "I'm not sure." I sucked the crumbs off my fingertip. I couldn't bring myself to tell him I would compete with him for the part. I mean, he might be mad at me like that time I drank the rest of his soda when he went to the bathroom at the movies. I wondered how actors in Hollywood stayed friends when they auditioned for the same roles.

Mrs. Harrington walked by, munching on an Eggo.

"Hey, Mrs. Harrington," I hollered, "can I ask you something?" *Nice projection*, I thought to myself. I would need to pump myself up for the audition, since hardly anyone else knew.

"What do you need, boys?" She stood at the edge of the table, biting off another hunk of Eggo. *Crrrunch, crunch, crunch.*

"We want to know more about the play," I said.

"We *do*?" Marquis looked at me, confused.

A shower of golden Eggo crumbs rained down on Mrs. Harrington's gray sweatshirt. "Then you'll be happy to know we're spending the period talking about the play today." She picked at an Eggo chunk lodged in her teeth with her fingernail and spun around.

"Thank YOU, Mrs. Harring-TAWN!" I called after her, trying to be more expressive. Which sounded odd, so . . .

"Why you talking like that?" Marquis asked.

"Like *whaaaat, old chap*?" I tried on a British accent, which sounded even odder. Splendidly odd, I'd say, by Jove.

"You sounded like a British robot." Marquis twisted up his face. I worried he was getting suspicious.

"I'm. Just being EXPRESSIVE!" I shot my arm out to the right, like I'd seen Mrs. Darling and Janie do earlier.

"All righty, then." Marquis stood, dusting his hands off. "Let's get to class before you express yourself to the office."

Okay, boss, whatever you say, I thought. I wondered if Marquis was trying to psych me out. Now *I* was the one who was suspicious.

As I followed behind, my stomach cramped and reminded me I was the dishonest one.

~~~

Later that morning in English, I sat up straight in my chair, ready to listen to Mrs. Harrington start talking about the play.

"What's up with you today, Zack?" Marquis asked.

"Yeah, what're you thinking about in that head of yours, Zack?" Janie added.

"I just want to hear about the play." I shrugged, leaning back, trying to play it off. "That's all."

"Why?" they both said in unison, like they were auditioning for backup singers.

The bell rang.

"Sophia!" Stepping from behind her desk, Mrs. Harrington snapped on like a light switch. We turned.

Sitting on a chair near the reading rug we never used, Sophia generously smeared gray eye shadow on one of the blue-eye-shadow gang (what I called the girls who follow her around, doing what she does, which is usually wearing clumps of sky blue eye shadow). A short line had formed. As they waited their turn with Sophia, they flipped though magazines. It looked like Sophia's Beauty Shop was having its grand opening.

Sophia stood back, motioning at the line. "I'm kinda slammed right now," she replied. "I'll get back to you later, Mrs. Harrington."

"No, Sophia, you will get back to me *now*!" Mrs. Harrington's sensible shoes squeaked as she stepped to the back of the room. "This needs to stop now!"

"*Uuuugh!* What, Miss?" Sophia clicked her tongue. "I got to practice my makeup skills for the play."

"How is giving the girls in my class smoky eyes helping with the play?" Mrs. Harrington demanded.

"Okay, first of all . . ." Sophia turned, resting her hand on her hip. "Mrs. Darling said I needed to do more than blue eye shadow and lip gloss." She held up and wiggled the gray eye shadow case. "Soooo . . ."

"Did she now?" Mrs. Harrington crossed her arms, pulling her chin back.

"And you always say we have to write to get better at writing, so I'm makeuping to get better at makeuping." Sophia explained. She had a point. You know, Sophia really can make whatever she wants to do sound like it's the right thing. "So I'm really just doing what you said, if you think about it."

"*Riiiight?*" The smoky-eye-shadow line chimed in, looking up from their magazines.

Mrs. Harrington sighed, defeated. "Okay, makeup for the play *only*. But no magazines during class."

"*Aww,* Miss, it's free-choice reading!" But they knew not to push Mrs. Harrington. She obviously wasn't in the mood to battle with Sophia's logic. Honestly, I wanted the interruptions to stop too, because I needed information about the play to give me an edge. Then I thought about it. José and Marquis would get the same information. But then I remembered José never listens. I was rocking it odd up in here. I was my own hype man! *Wha'? Wha'?*

"Just make sure you listen at least," Mrs. Harrington said. "Can you do that?"

"*I'll* make sure they listen." Blythe stood and pushed the cardigan sleeves off her hands and pulled out her notebook, as if she were getting ready to write a ticket.

"I will, too," Chewy said, scurrying to stand. He leaned toward me and whispered, "Can I have some paper?"

I ripped out a piece and handed it to him.

Blythe approached.

"And a pencil?" Chewy whispered again.

I sighed and gave him a pencil.

Blythe fronted Chewy, like a cardigan-clad theater bully. Chewy shrank away, backing into his seat, mouthing *Sorry!* again to Blythe.

"We've got an audition to prepare for, people." Blythe snapped her notebook on her hand so hard she flinched.

"Sit down, Blythe!" Mrs. Harrington quashed the last interruption. Finally. I leaned in as she uncapped a purple marker and wrote *Scrooge* on a piece of chart paper. I could barely sit still. She'd have to tell us more than the three sentences I'd found online last night. Get this? It's a ghost story *and* a Christmas story. This Charles Dickens guy must have been like the LEGO movies of his time. Everybody loved his books.

"I thought you were going to explain about *A Christmas Carol* today," Cliché whined.

"She's TRYING to!" I snapped, a little too expressively. Cliché shot me the stink eye.

"Thank you, Mr. Delacruz." Mrs. Harrington smiled. I noticed Marquis looking at me side-eyed.

"As I was saying"—Mrs. Harrington's shoes squeaked across the room—"Scrooge is one of the most well-known characters in all of literature."

Bythe's pen scratched across her notebook page.

"And Scrooge is the main character of this play." Abhi knew things. I only wish I'd been able to talk to her more on the bus yesterday—or on the phone. But I didn't have her digits.

"Yes, and what do we know about main characters?" Mrs. Harrington continued.

"They're important?" I answered, but it sounded like a question.

"They're the stars of the play," José strutted to the front of the room, bowing. "Hold your applause," he said, humbly holding his hand out. "Please."

Hey! That's my line! You can ask Mom's cabinets.

"I can put this fire out, ma'am," Blythe offered. "As stage manager, I feel I need to step up when the assistant director doesn't." She glared at Chewy.

"Zip it, Blythe," Mrs. Harrington barked, "You're not helping at all." But honestly, it did seem like Mrs. Harrington needed some assistance.

"One last thing." El blew a big kiss to our English class.

Mrs. Harrington and I shared a sigh. She was trying to teach us, and I was trying to learn.

"Go ahead." I leaned forward, my elbows propped on my desk.

"What else do you remember about main characters and the literary elements?" Mrs. Harrington asked.

"What did you call me?" El looked at the class, waiting for laughter, but this time he had no takers. *"Justkidding."*

Lately, Mrs. Harrington had been on a real literary elements kick—you know, *setting, conflict, characters.* Davy Crockett Middle School was full of literary elements—it had *obstacles, plot twists,* and *antagonists.*

Mrs. Harrington sat on her stool and read from something she'd printed off the Internet. "The main characters often change the most. *A Christmas Carol* shows how interacting with the other characters in different settings changes Scrooge from a lonely, grouchy miser to a caring, giving human."

"I'm caring." I sat up.

"And I'm a *my*-ser or a *yours*-er or whatever." El nodded. "Whatever you just said, I am that."

"Miser," Mrs. Harrington corrected. "I said *miser*."

"That's what I said," José replied, looking at Abhi for confirmation. "Didn't I?"

"I'm grouchy," Blythe announced. It was official. With one new job assignment, she'd gone from most irritatingly *happy* bossy girl to most irritatingly *grouchy* bossy girl. Characters weren't the only ones who change, that's for sure.

"Marquis is giving," Cliché added, causing Marquis to shrug and smile uncomfortably.

Was that really necessary? Et tu, Cliché?

I needed so many answers. *How do best friends go out for the same role? What's the Internet say about that, Mrs. Harrington? I mean, you want for your friend to get what he wants, right? That's being a good friend. But what about when you both want the same thing? You kind of want yourself to get it more.* At least I did.

When I thought about it, it didn't sound like I was caring or much of a friend. I was secretive and only out for myself to get the role. I was the *antagonist*—the *villain*—or perhaps the star. I wanted to feel what it was like to be the numero uno of Motivational Poster City.

Daydreaming, I looked over at Marquis, who smiled, which made me feel even worse.

CHAPTER 9
STAR QUALITY

Y ou know, I've been thinking." Marquis tilted his head to the side. "I'm not so sure the Scrooge part's for me."

Did I hear that right?

"You know. You'd make a great Bob Cratchit," Cliché advised, practically telling Marquis *not* to try out for Scrooge. She must've thought someone else should be Scrooge, but she wanted to save Marquis the disappointment of not getting the role. Cliché was so nice to Marquis, letting him down easy like that.

"I can see that." Mrs. Harrington nodded. Wow! Even Mrs. Harrington didn't think Marquis should be Scrooge.

"Who's this Bob Cratchit dude?" Marquis asked.

"He's Scrooge's clerk, who works really hard, and

Scrooge doesn't pay him enough money to feed his family," Janie added.

"That Scrooge character sounds mean," Marquis said.

It's true, I thought to myself.

Wait.

Maybe I was becoming a selfish Scrooge, who wanted to keep the best role all to himself.

"I've got star quality, am I right?" José interrupted.

"Of course you do, El." Abhi smiled. "Your eyes practically sparkle."

"Awe!" José gazed at his reflection in the window. "They do, don't they?"

I gritted my teeth. I forgot about El *Problemo* Loco. He strolled over and handed Blythe a permission slip to take the late bus, like we'd all done earlier this morning in the cafeteria.

It couldn't be. I had counted on El forgetting his permission slip.

Blythe checked it over. "This is acceptable, but tell your mother to take more time with her signature in the future."

"What'd you say about my mom?" El spun around.

"DON'T push me, Mr. Loco."

"*Justkidding.*" José danced back to his seat.

He's an agile foe, this one. He's adapted and become just responsible enough to return his permission slip. José is an unexpected obstacle to my getting the part of Scrooge. I can adapt, too. But what could I do about El *Problemo* Loco?

"Actually, I think the ghosstss are the real sstars," Janie stood.

"Did you say 'ghosstss'?" El sprayed spit at Janie. "*Jussssttkidding.*"

"Yes," Janie continued, not allowing El to throw her off her game. I admired that. "The three ghostsss are the main characters to me."

"Tell me more, Janie," Mrs. Harrington said from a stool.

"They make Scrooge realize he has to change." Janie numbered the ghosts off on her fingers as she named them: "The Ghost of Christmas Past, the Ghost of Christmas Present, and the Ghost of Christmas Future."

"Hold up!" José did a double take. "Nobody said anything about there being grammar in this play."

"Grammar?" Janie squinted.

"You know, past, present, and future—that sounds like grammar." José shuddered.

"No way," Janie explained. "They're the ghostss's *names*, not *verb tenses*." Smiling, Janie stepped toward José. "Like the Ghost of Christmas Past is from when Scrooge was a kid, and—"

"Ghosts?" Blythe glared at Mrs. Harrington. "*You* didn't say there were ghosts."

"I literally haven't had a chance," Mrs. Harrington said. And she really hadn't.

"So I'll be manager of ghosts, too?" Blythe eyes widened. "Who would have believed?" She started scribbling something in her notebook, laughing like a cartoon villainess.

"Mrs. Harrington, if there are really ghosts, I can't be in the play." Cliché shook her head. "My mom says

50

the only ghost I'll ever be around is the holy one." Cliché made the sign of the cross, and put her head down on the desk.

"Maybe you could call your mom and ask," Abhi offered, always thinking about others. Maybe I didn't deserve to be friends with Abhi. Maybe I was like Scrooge.

"Okay," Mrs. Harrington sighed. "Use the phone at my desk. But quickly."

"I'll tell you why else this play needs the ghosts." Janie waved an invitation for everybody to come closer. We complied, because Janie was the expert on *A Christmas Carol* and ghosts. Maybe I should have called *her* last night.

Janie continued, "The Ghost of Christmas Past takes Scrooge to remind him how Christmas was when he was a kid."

We nodded, listening to her every word.

"And then, the Ghost of Christmas Present shows Scrooge how bad Christmas is for the Cratchits now. They don't have enough to eat or to take care of their sick child, Tiny Tim."

"That's sad," El said.

"Yes, El, it is," Janie agreed. "But it gets worse. To make sure Scrooge changes, the Ghost of Christmas Future shows Scrooge how horrible it will be for the Cratchits in the future if Scrooge doesn't change his miserly ways."

We clapped when we thought Janie had finished.

"That's why the ghosts are so important." Janie swooped her arms around like Mrs. Darling. "They bring all the drama. They're like the whole plot—conflict, rising action, climax, resolution—they're everything!"

Mrs. Harrington clapped along, delighted that her literary elements unit had reached someone.

"No ghosts? No play." The unstoppable Janie was unstoppable.

"Yes," Abhi took over. Finally. "And because of what Scrooge sees, he changes and becomes generous instead of staying selfish."

I loved the sound of Abhi's voice. I mean Janie's is okay, but Abhi's voice is smooth like soft-serve ice cream from the Golden Corral. When I listened to Abhi, I wanted to become generous instead of selfish.

"God bless us, every one!" Janie jumped in and finished the summary. "Which, BTDubbs, is the last line of the movie version of *A Christmas Carol*, spoken by none other than Tiny Tim."

"And scene!" Blythe shouted and stood. "Good show, everyone!"

"But that's my jo—" Chewy began, trailing off midsentence when Blythe's eyes met his.

"My uncle has a friend named Tiny." Cliché hung up the phone. "But he's enormous! Is Tiny Tim *actually* tiny or is he the *opposite* of tiny, like Tiny?"

Mrs. Harrington's mouth hung slack. "Uh . . ."

"I got this," Abhi said. "He's tiny—or short."

Who'd want *that* part, I wondered. I sat up straighter to look as *un*tiny as I could. I wanted to be Scrooge. No way I wanted to be the short kid. I've already had that role, and I'm ready for *that* one to go to someone else.

A s soon as the final bell rang, hopeful auditioners swarmed the cafeteria like ants. "Technically," Mrs. Darling had explained earlier, "even though we call it the cafeteria, it's actually a cafetorium. It's a combination of a *cafeteria* and an *auditorium*." A full stage setup with lights and everything hides behind thick curtains. It's been a cafetorium all this time. Who knew? Smells of Comet cleaner and burritos mingled as I sized up my competition. El Pollo Loco was the only one who had been committed to the part of Scrooge the whole time. Committed like I've never seen him. I wondered if anyone else wanted to be Scrooge. Most of the sixth grade roamed around, chatting in front of the stage, waiting. My stomach tightened and I forgot to breathe for a second.

I probably should have taken it as a bad sign that no

seventh- or eighth-graders showed up for the audition. What did they know that we didn't? That's called *foreshadowing*. We learned about that literary element in Mrs. Harrington's class the other day. *Foreshadowing* is a hint in a story that something bad or good is going to happen later in the story. Thing is, my life is full of foreshadowing— little hints of what's to come. An overcrowded audition. No adult supervision as yet, and my stomach gurgling. Again. But I wasn't listening to the bad signs—or gurgles. I chose the odd path—the path of the opposite. I flipped the switch on my fear and plowed forward, thinking positively, a walking motivational poster.

"This is so exciting," Abhi stood next to me.

"I kn—" I began.

"Everyone quiet down!" Blythe ordered, pushing up her cardigan sleeves, walking around like she was Coach O. in gym. "This isn't chitchat time; it's show time."

"But that's *my* job," Chewy whined.

"Well, like my daddy always says, 'Blythe steps in when leadership is lacking.'" Blythe opened her eyes wide and clicked her pen.

Chewy gripped a clipboard and a sharpened yellow pencil with a new pink eraser. At least he had his supplies. That was an improvement.

"Please take a seat," Chewy said firmly.

Abhi sat first. I sat on her left and El on her right. Cliché and Marquis filled in the table.

"Where's Janie?" Cliché asked. As we looked around in the momentary silence, my stomach gurgled and bubbled like an unclogging drain. *Gluuuuuuf.* It stopped and everyone looked around, wondering what they'd just heard. I felt my bowel growl erupting again. My conflict: burrito vs. stomach.

Abhi's face pinched. "What *was* that?"

"Sounds like little D has the big D." El Doctoro Loco diagnosed. I waited for him to add "*justkidding.*" But not this time.

"Uh," I said, a mist of sweat beading on my forehead. My stomach interrupted: *Glurf, glurf, glurfupple. Blub, bluppht. . . .*

"Wait for it," El Pollo Loco said.

Glug.

"And uh one more time!" José stood, pointing at my stomach.

Glug.

"I think we all better turtle up." El pulled his shirt collar up over his mouth and nose. "Zack's tummy is *foreshadowing* a fart."

Even Marquis burst out laughing.

"Do you need to go to the restroom, Zack?" Abhi asked, being helpful.

"Yeah, Zack, do you need to pinch a loaf, or is it still baking?" El asked, NOT being helpful.

Marquis changed the subject from my bubble guts. "So, I am trying out for Bob Cratchit. Who're y'all trying out for?"

"I'm going to be Scrooge!" José announced. Then he began chanting, "Diarrhea, Diarrhea! When you're walking through the store, and there's cleanup on aisle four . . ."

My eyes scoured the cafetorium for a sign of Mrs. Darling. *Glurf, glurf.*

"Diarrhea, Diarrhea!" Chewy joined El's chant, beating out a rhythm on his clipboard with a pencil.

El continued, "When you have to change your stance, cuz cottage cheese just filled your pants . . ."

Suddenly, Chewy dropped his clipboard on a table and ran.

In Chewy's absence, Blythe attempted to direct the crowd by turning the cafetorium lights on and off. But they got stuck in the OFF position. From the dark backstage, Blythe yelled, "Never fear. I shall give you light!" But you could hear a frustrated doubt in her grunts. The darkness swallowed us up.

Suddenly, the metal doors burst open. A shadowy figure appeared. Light bled in from the windows, revealing a white blobbish figure. The unidentifiable mass inched toward us.

"It's a ghost!" Cliché screamed.

Marquis screeched and dropped to the floor with a thud.

"It's a ghost, not a tornado!" Cliché shrieked.

All at once, we realized that the ghost was creeping toward us. "AHHHHHH! GHOST!"

"What's that horrible scraping noise?" Cliché cried.

Chains dragged behind the whitish mass. We backed away, inching toward the other side of the cafetorium, the doors, and escape.

"OUT, spirit!" Cliché threw her hands up and spoke with conviction like a preacher. "OUT! In the name of all things holy!"

The white blobby ghost lurched toward us.

"Please, Blythe!" Marquis yelled. "Turn on the lights before it's too late!"

"People, what do you think I'm trying to do?" Blythe barked. "Sheesh!"

"TURN ON THE LIGHTS!"

"I'm not turning the lights back on until you're all quiet!" Blythe screamed. "I'm the stage manager, people!" Her voice deepened. "I will not be ignored!"

The blob scraped closer.

A blast of light burst from above, blinding us. Mountains of sheets covered a moving figure trudging toward us. The lights only helped us see the approaching horror. The Ghost dragged a big black bowling ball on a chain. Half of the auditioners poured out the emergency exits at the back of the cafetorium, screaming bloody murder.

"Wait! Mr. Akins, please tell the buses to wait!"

"We've gotta get out of here, man!"

"Theater club is weird!"

The exit doors slammed. An arm reached from beneath the cloth and ripped away the sheet that covered its head. But instead of a skinless skull, Janie Bustamante's head appeared.

"The ghosssstsss have arrived," Janie announced to the few students remaining. She took a deep and dramatic bow. "I'm here for the audition."

CHAPTER 11
BAH! HUMBUG!

"**W**ell, that's one way to get rid of the competition," Blythe said to Janie.

"I'm a method actress!" Janie replied, trying to sit, but suddenly realizing the number of sheets tangled about her wouldn't allow it.

"If by *method*, you mean wrapping yourself in sheets." Blythe smirked.

"Oh, my!" Mrs. Darling entered, sipping a diet soda straight from the can like she was in a commercial. She gave Janie the once-over. "Janie, you do know how to make an entrance."

"Thank you!" Janie nodded, caressing her sheets as if they were the finest prom dress. "I got such a deal on all these used sheets at Goodwill, and the bowling ball was only one dollar!"

We stood in shocked silence.

Janie yanked on the chain tied around the bowling ball, wobbling it forward. Odd was perfectly normal for Janie. But somehow she pulled it off.

Mrs. Darling's eyes glazed over as she drank in the entirety of Janie's costume, like she'd been put in a trance. Suddenly, she jerked awake.

"Where's Chewy?" Mrs. Darling asked.

"Here I am." He walked back in, drying his hands on a paper towel. "Now?"

"No time like the present."

Chewy picked up his clipboard off the table. Mrs. Darling paced, smiling at what was left of the auditioners, scattered across a few lunch tables. "Bravo! Brava! Thespians! Such a wonderful turnout. I'll have to make some tough choices today, won't I, Chewy?"

"Uh-huh." Chewy gripped his clipboard. "All right, I'm Chewy Johnson, the assistant director for the Actin' Alamos' annual production of *A Christmas Carol*." Chewy took charge. Clipboards must give off a magic power of authority to whoever holds them. "I will call the role name, then who'll be reading for it." Chewy cleared his throat. "First up, the lead role of Ebenezer Scrooge: Marquis Malone, Zack Delacruz, and José Soto."

I popped my head toward Marquis at the exact moment he popped his at me.

I guess Marquis changed his mind. But he would've told me. Wouldn't he?

Marquis looked at me like I had used the last bit of his mechanical pencil lead. "Zack?"

"Zack, look at you!" Janie chuckled. "Why were you holding back?"

"Yeah, Zack," Marquis demanded. "Why?"

Everybody looked shocked that I was on the list for Scrooge.

Marquis, José, and I scooted out of our chairs and moved toward the stage. Marquis and I climbed the stairs. José, in El Pollo Loco style, leapt over the steps, springing up like a gymnast and landing on my foot.

"Ouch!" I shoved El away.

"On *my* stage, we use the steps!" Blythe's voice growled from the dark wings on the side of the stage. Blythe really had settled into the villainess role.

José flinched, gazing into the dark unknown of the wings.

Chewy had called a few other names too, but they had been smart enough to *not* show up. Or they could've rushed out screaming when they thought Janie was a ghost attacking us.

If I did get the part of Ebenezer Scrooge, everything in my life would change forever. No more lonely afternoons. Instead I'd be at play rehearsals with my friends. And I'd be a star with a real audience of living, breathing people—not appliances.

Hands behind her back, Mrs. Darling paced in front of the stage as the three of us stood in a row, side by side by side.

"Gentlemen," Mrs. Darling began, "Mr. Scrooge is an A-1 grouch, and I want you to give me your best Grumpy Gus. Leave it all on the stage, as they say."

Marquis raised his hand.

"Yes, Marquis?"

"I want to be Mr. Scrooge's employee, Bob Cratchit, not Mr. Scrooge." Marquis shrugged. "I'd like the role to go to Zack or José."

I shot a look at Marquis.

"But mostly Zack." Marquis smiled, zipping his baby-blue warm-up zipper up and down.

"Would you, now?" Mrs. Darling squinted, massaging her temples. "Tell you what. I'm the director, and I choose who gets what parts, so if you don't mind, Marquis, I'd like to get on with this audition."

Marquis's eyes widened.

Blythe emerged from the dark wings and gave Mrs. Darling two thumbs up and a wink. Then she disappeared again, leaving behind a faint smell of baby powder.

"Okay." Marquis shrugged at me.

It was just the three of us competing for what Abhi thought was the most important role—Marquis, *man vs. best friend*; and José, *hombre vs. pollo, man vs. chicken*.

"First, you will be asked to say Ebenezer Scrooge's trademark phrase." She stopped pacing, took in a breath, and said in a deep voice. "Bah! Humbug!"

Huh?

Confused, José, Marquis, and I looked at each other. Neither Mrs. Harrington, nor the Internet, nor Janie had mentioned whatever Mrs. Darling had said. I couldn't figure out what words she was saying. *Baa* is like a sheep, right? Nobody said anything about sheep either.

"Bah! Humbug!" Mrs. Darling repeated. "Say it, José."

José stepped forward, clasping his hands behind his back. "Bad *ham*burger!"

Everybody cracked up, and José bowed.

"Zack?" Mrs. Darling crossed her arms and waited. It was like I was hearing underwater and her voice was all garbled.

"Bad. HAND Bag?" I eeked out, softly and slowly, and not like a Grumpy Gus at all. My throat closed, and my stomach growled loud enough to sound like the school had plumbing issues.

"Marquis?"

Marquis cleared his throat. "Bah! Humbug!" For somebody who didn't want the role, he sounded an awful lot like a Grumpy Gus.

"Splendid, Marquis! Okay." Mrs. Darling massaged her temples. She paced. "Let's try something else, boys."

CHAPTER 12
A MEMORABLE EXIT

Mrs. Darling slipped off her gold sandals, setting free her granny-finger toes. This was getting serious.

Chewy and those sitting nearby rushed away, escaping the sandals' stinky-cheese aroma.

"In this scene, Scrooge's nephew visits; he is the absolute cheery opposite of Scrooge."

"That's conflict," Janie blurted. "Person versus person."

Mesmerized, I watched Mrs. Darling's long toes grip the linoleum like a bird of prey. I *toe*-tally wasn't listening again, but I did hear the last part of her directions. "One of those happy, happy people."

"Like you, Mrs. Darling?" José batted his overly long eyelashes.

Oh, brother.

"I suppose." Mrs. Darling continued. "He's all *Merry*

Christmas this and *Merry Christmas that* and Scrooge is all *Bah! humbug*—the grumbling, grousy grouch." She paced again and stopped, her toes curled like they were gripping a large branch. I tried to look away, but I couldn't.

"In the lines we are going to read, Ebenezer Scrooge has had enough of his nephew's Christmas cheer. Scrooge says *good afternoon* over and over, trying to get his gleeful nephew to leave his office. He's basically saying, 'Goodbye,' so the nephew would take his cheerful self elsewhere."

Mrs. Darling stopped pacing again, sat on a chair, and rubbed her talons, pulling each one out till it popped. That's all I could pay attention *toe*—I mean *to*. As she massaged her feet, her toes went every which way, looking like a squid in its underwater habitat.

I think she said something about changing how Scrooge says *good afternoon* each time. I had no idea what she was talking about, because I'd been unable to take my eyes off her undulating toes.

"Each has to be different, more and more angry each time. More and more over the top. Mr. Delacruz," Mrs. Darling said, smiling, "You're up first."

"Good after . . ." I tried to say it, but it got caught in my throat like a wad of bubble gum.

"You're not projecting, Zack!" Mrs. Darling motioned behind her. "You must say it to the back of the cafetorium. Pretend you are throwing your voice like a baseball to the back of the room." She peered over her lime-green half-glasses. "Understand?"

I nodded. But I didn't understand. How was my voice a baseball? Plus, I don't throw baseballs that well anyway.

I looked to Abhi for comfort. She smiled. I got the shot of energy I needed.

"GOOD AFTERNOO-*o*-O-*o*!" I yelled. My voice broke like a glass bottle shattering against a brick wall. At least it had traveled to the back of the room.

Everybody laughed.

Mrs. Darling smiled. "That might be good for the last one. You really don't have anywhere to go after that, do you?"

Was it too late for me? I was all up in my head and doubting myself. I shook my head, shrugging. I didn't know what to do, but then I blurted out, "Good afternoon!"

I figured it was loud enough when Mrs. Darling ended the uncomfortable silence. "Mr. Malone, give it a shot."

Marquis stepped to the center of the stage. With mathematical precision he said his lines: "Good AFTERnoon. Good afterNOON! GOOOD AFTER-NOON!"

"Perfect volume and variety!" Mrs. Darling said, "but where was the passion? The raw feeling?"

"Huh?" Marquis asked.

"Where's your anger?"

Marquis considered her question. "I don't think I have any anger, Mrs. Darling."

"Very well. Mr. Soto, please give it a try." Mrs. Darling continued pacing.

"Good afterNOON!" José yelled.

"Now, that's raw!" Mrs. Darling beamed. "Nice use of your vocal instrument, José."

"GOOOOD afternoon!" José really did sound peeved.

65

"Bring it home, El!" Mrs. Darling stopped pacing.

And then José crossed the stage. "I said, GOOD *DAY*!" And he stomped out the stage door and slammed it shut.

The crowd of auditioners stood, applauding loudly, even cheering.

Blythe had to let José back in for his standing ovation.

What? Scrooge is not supposed to leave. The nephew is. And he left the building. Shouldn't that disqualify his audition? That didn't even make sense!

"And . . . scene! Now *that's* acting!" Mrs. Darling applauded. "My, my, my, José. When you channel your energy and creativity, you're unstoppable."

Blythe emerged from the dark wings. "Please note. The stage door is not a prop, but a safety exit only to be used at my direction."

I stood on the side of the stage, like a soda that had lost all its fizz. Abhi smiled and clapped for El Pollo Loco, too. Our eyes met, and she held her thumb up. But was that for me or for El?

CHAPTER 13
ALL THREE?

Thud. *BANG!*
   Thud. BANG!
   Thud. BANG!

As Janie climbed the stage stairs, her bowling ball followed one step behind.

Mrs. Darling massaged her temples—again. "Is there no one else besides Janie who wants to try out for the Ghost of Christmas Past or the Ghost of Christmas Present?" she pleaded. "The Ghost of Christmas Future? *Anyone?*" Her green eyes scanned the small group of auditioners.

"No one else besides Janie signed up, Mrs. Darling," Chewy replied, tapping his pencil on his clipboard of courage. "I guess all of her enthusiasm for the ghosts scared other people off, and she was already in costume."

Then Cliché stood.

"Oh, wonderful! Cliché dear, step up to the stage," Mrs. Darling gushed.

"No, ma'am." Cliché shook her head. "My mom said I could be in the play, but I couldn't be a ghost."

Mrs. Darling sighed.

"Who you gonna call?" Janie bellowed. "From the motion picture *Ghostbusters*, nineteen eighty-four and twenty sixteen, starring a young Bill Murray and a hilarious Kate McKinnon, respectively."

Mrs. Darling gazed at her script, making a note. "Are you ready to read for the Ghost of Christmas Past, Present, or Yet to Come?"

Janie played with the chain, knocking the bowling ball around. "I checked out the play from the public library, and I memorized all three parts last night."

"Well, that's certainly some Actin' Alamos ambition." Mrs. Darling smiled.

"Can I be all three ghosstsss, Mrs. Darling?" Janie begged. "I promise I'll bring something new to each role. I see the Ghost of Christmas Past all . . ." Janie draped the sheet on top of her head, holding it together below her chin, looking like she was ready for a windstorm.

Then, she wrapped a sheet around her shoulders and changed her voice. "And Ghost of Christmas Present all in a shawl, y'all." She turned again. "And I see Ghost of—"

"That'll do, Janie," Mrs. Darling interrupted. "You'll find out Monday morning along with everyone else when I post the cast list on the library door."

"But I have another look you haven't seen yet!"

"I've seen enough. Truly, dear."

"Nailed it!" Janie fist-pumped. "My Aunt Monica said it was in the stars that I'd be all three ghosts." Janie jumped off the stage and the bowling ball crashed on the tile floor, bouncing out of control, narrowly missing Mrs. Darling's bare talons. I guess that near accident foreshadowed events yet to come, but I don't think anybody thought twice about it then. It was Janie, after all.

Marquis and several other boys tried out for Bob Cratchit, and of course Cliché tried out for *Mrs.* Cratchit. I didn't try out for any other roles, but at one point, Mrs. Darling told Marquis, Cliché, and me to stand together in a row. She turned her head side to side, squinting, and moved her gaze from Marquis to Cliché and then to me.

"Cliché," Mrs. Darling said, "I don't need you anymore. Take a seat."

Cliché sat, crossing her arms.

"Abhi," Mrs. Darling called. "I'd like to see how you look with these two."

"Mrs. Darling, this script seems short." Blythe appeared from the wings.

"Good eye, dear." She moved me to the left, then the right, on either side of Marquis and Abhi. "I have created a special adaptation the show, so it runs no longer than sixty minutes. We perform it once for all the sixth-, seventh-, and eighth-graders at the end of the day on Friday before winter holiday."

Mr. Akins walked in and stood at the back of the cafetorium. "Mrs. Darling, I hate to interrupt, but the late bus is here. We must seek to bring this audition to a close."

She looked at the clock, which read almost 5. I couldn't believe time went by so quickly. "Oh, dear! It is getting late, Actin' Alamos."

"But we haven't read for all the parts yet," Chewy said.

"Never fear, thespians, I have enough information to make my cast and crew decisions." Mrs. Darling cleared her throat, which meant *case closed*.

I thought I knew what she meant. But I had no idea.

None. At. All.

Sunday night, back at Dad's house, every time I rolled over in bed, this whole audition thing ended differently. I plot-twisted all night. Twisting one way, I got the part of Scrooge. I grinned and everybody patted me on the back. Then, I'd roll over the other way, and I'd find out I wouldn't be in the play at all, and I'd spend endless weeks of unshared snacks, just *Judge Joe* and me, waiting alone for Dad or Mom to come home. And then I pressed the pillow over my ears, struggling to silence my thoughts.

Dad woke me Monday morning by yanking off my comforter. For a brief moment, I felt sure I was Scrooge. But then my fate kept turning over and over in my mind like my sleepless night.

As we Actin' Alamos walked from the bus circle to break-fast, we continued our conversations about the auditions, as we'd done on the bus Friday. We predicted who'd get what part, and everyone asked for feedback on how they'd done on stage. Except for me. I kept quiet. I wasn't sure what odd behavior was anymore. I just felt odd.

When we walked in the cafeteria doors, Mrs. Gage stood guard by the milk cart. "Can we go to the library to see the cast list, Mrs. Gage?" Cliché asked. She had been appointed to ask for the group.

"Nobody is going anywhere until you get a tray and eat everything on it," Mrs. Gage insisted.

We raced through the breakfast line, grabbing a sausage roll, a juice box, and a carton of milk from the metal cart. The auditioners sat together and chowed down. We were already a group, and that felt pretty good.

"Well, I'm pretty sure she's going to choose me thrice." Janie tore off a bite of her sausage roll. "I'm a ghossstsss' ghost."

"The ghostest with the mostest," I said.

Everybody laughed, and Janie smiled at me.

"Do ghosts talk with their mouths full?" Cliché chided. "If so, then you're a shoo-in."

Janie turned and glared a response at Cliché, chewing violently.

"No ma'am." Cliché shook her head, wagging her finger. "Don't you chew that sausage roll at me."

"Do you think I did a good job reading the part of Bob

Cratchit?" Marquis, the peacemaker, changed the subject.

"Yeeees," Cliché answered, tilting her head. And he had. Unfortunately for me, he read well for Bob Cratchit *and* Ebenezer Scrooge. I nodded, thinking and gnawing on my sausage roll. I ate all the bread first and saved the sausage—my favorite part—for last. I wondered if I'd done what I needed to do in the auditions. Was I loud enough? I know I finished stronger than I began. But that's only because I started so weak.

When breakfast was almost over, José and Abhi walked up to the table.

"Was I cheerful enough?" Marquis asked.

"The cheeriest." Cliché put down her sausage roll on the tray and leaned toward Marquis. "You were the best actor on that stage yesterday."

"Oh, I'm going to be sick!" José pretended to barf, with sound effects and all.

"Maybe you should sit somewhere else then," Cliché snapped, stiffening her back, still mad at Abhi for also auditioning for Mrs. Cratchit.

"Oh, we'll be fine," Abhi sat. "Thank you for your concern, Cliché."

"Oh, it's such a shame." Cliché shook her head.

"What is?" Abhi opened her milk.

"Too bad you're not finished with your breakfast," Cliché explained, "so you won't be able to go with us to see the cast and crew list."

Marquis's and my eyes met.

"Mrs. Gage's rule; not mine." Cliché shrugged, standing up. "Let's make like a tree and leaf!"

All at once, Abhi's swigged the carton of milk, dropped it on the table, and slammed her hand down, flattening the carton, with a bang. Impressed, I was. Abhi stood with us, pushed back a burp, and followed. "I'm vegetarian, so I don't eat sausage."

José grabbed his roll and hers and stuffed them in his mouth, one in each cheek. He looked like a chipmunk from the woodland biome.

"Well, to be fair," Chewy added, "There may not actually be any meat in it."

"What Mrs. Gage doesn't know won't hurt her." Abhi's tossed her Styrofoam tray in the garbage.

We walked briskly. As we rounded the first corner, we sprinted, as if we were running for our lives, and in a way, we were. Our whole future rested on what roles we'd been given. In a hushed silence, we gathered around the door to read the cast and crew list, pushing on each other to get close enough to read it.

I only wanted one part.

A few seconds later, I saw my fate. I saw my role. And it knocked the wind out of me. I *wasn't* Scrooge.

But I was given a role. The role no short person would ever want. Not in a million, zillion years. A sharp pain stabbed my stomach. There it was in black and white, my role: Tiny Tim. I stood in stunned silence while voices of celebration and surprise splashed over me like a salty wave of embarrassment. I wanted to float out to sea, captured by the cruel current of the ocean biome. I stood motionless, like driftwood, washed ashore with no current to move it.

A CHRISTMAS CAROL

Adapted for the Actin' Alamos

Cafetorium Stage

by J. Darling, MIS

CAST

Ebenezer Scrooge .... José Soto

Ghosts of Christmas
Past, Present, and Future .... Janie Bustamante

Bob Cratchit .... Marquis Malone

Mrs. Cratchit .... Abhi Bhatt

Tiny Tim .... Zack Delacruz

Niece .... Cliché Jones

Alternates ....Zack Delacruz, Cliché Jones

CREW

Director .... Judith Darling

Assistant Director .... Chewy Johnson

Stage Manager and Prop Mistress ..... Blythe Balboa

Makeup .... Sophia Segura

CHAPTER 15
THE ROLE OF DEFEAT

"You won't even need to act to play *your* part, Zack!" El Pollo Loco taunted.

"YOU won't have to act!" I snapped back before I realized how lame my comeback was.

"But you're an alternate, too, Zack," Blythe offered. "That's a very important role." She motioned her head at José. "In case someone has to drop out of the play . . . for whatever reason." Blythe winked.

I nodded. But I didn't want the role I'd been given.

"Where's my name?" Cliché asked.

"You're an alternate, too. And the niece," Janie offered. "That's show biz. You take the part you're given."

"But I wanted to be Mrs. Cratchit," Cliché whined, giving Abhi a cold, hard stare.

"It's not Abhi's fault you didn't get the part you wanted, Cliché," Janie said.

"Well . . ." Cliché sighed, holding back a tear. "I guess we'll be alternates together, Zack."

"Sure." I hoped everybody would forget I had the short-guy role of Tiny Tim and think of me only as an *alternate*.

"Alternates are crucial," Abhi added. "You can be called on to play any of the parts, and you have to be ready. It's quite exciting. I was an alternate back in Minnesota, and I ended up in a starring role when the lead got mono and had to stay home for six weeks."

"One person's tragedy is another person's opportunity." Cliché stared ahead, nodding.

"Students!" Mr. Akins walked up. "Please seek to disperse and proceed to advisory."

"It's okay, Mr. Akins, I'm the stage manager." Blythe held her hand up. "I will get these students to advisory lickety-split."

Blythe placed her hand on Cliché's arm to guide her to advisory. Cliché yanked her arm away, but Blythe didn't let go of Cliché's sweater sleeve and it slid off her shoulder.

"No, ma'am," Cliché warned. "You better let go of my sweater right now, or . . ."

"Ladies!" Mr. Akins stepped toward them.

Blythe dropped the sleeve and looked back at a confused Mr. Akins. "Kids! Am I right?" She shrugged.

"Humph!" Cliché jerked her sleeve back on and we all went to advisory.

77

wwmw

In advisory, in the announcements, Mr. Akins talked about the play. Blythe brought it up in math, and Janie brought it up in science by asking Mr. Stankowitz if he believed in ghosts.

"It is my life's purpose"—Janie choked back a tear—"to convince you they do exist when you come see our production in two weeks."

"Raise your hand if you're going to be a part of the play," Mr. Stankowitz asked, so I had to explain I was an alternate and Tiny Tim.

"Tiny Tim is the *second* most famous character," Abhi added.

"You should be very proud, m'man." Marquis stacked on the pity pile.

"Mrs. Darling says there are no small parts, just small actors." Blythe jotted a note to herself.

"HA! Get it?" El interrupted. "Small actors? Zack?" El slapped his knee.

A note landed on my desk.

To: Tiny Tim. The *T*'s in Tiny Tim were both drawn as crutches on the outside of the note. *Cute.* (That was sarcastic, by the way. It's called a *tone*. And I definitely had a *tone*, or a way of feeling, toward this note.) I nonchalantly slid it off my desk into my lap.

wwmw

I opened the note later, while Mr. Stankowitz continued his PowerPoint presentation on the biomes of the Earth—

yesterday, wetlands; today deserts. I knew what deserts felt like. All my opportunities had dried up. I only had a small part—literally—no matter what anybody said. Tiny Tim was like the tiny cactus of roles, prickly for all sorts of reasons.

"Hey, that saguaro cactus on the screen looks like one of Tiny Tim's crutches," El said.

I sank in my chair, which made me look even shorter. Great!

"Mr. Stankowitz!" Blythe flailed her hand about like she'd ignited in flames.

"This better be about science." Mr. Stankowitz smoothed back a few greasy strands of hair left on the desert biome of his head.

"It is," Blythe assured Mr. Stankowitz. "Do you know how you can remember to make sure you don't spell *dessert* when you mean to spell *desert*? You always want more dessert, so *dessert* has more *S*'s."

"That's dumb," El said. Sometimes he just said what everyone else was thinking. That got me worried. If El made fun of my height, had El just said what other people were thinking? What *did* people actually think about me?

"Soto, stop it," Mr. Stankowitz said. "That's quite enough."

And on and on and on the slide show went, dry and desolate like the desert biome of my life.

CHAPTER 16
POINTS

In English, Mrs. Harrington wasn't in her usual place at the door to shake our hands. She busily slid all the desks in a big circle. "We're taking a talking quiz today on the literary elements. The circle will allow for more interaction," she explained.

Oh, brother.

"I thought it'd be fun if we had a conversation quiz."

Why do adults think adding a word like *conversation* to *quiz* will suddenly cause students to jump for joy?

When Mrs. Harrington didn't see any smiles, she added, "You won't have to write anything!"

Even I cracked a smile. Well played, Mrs. Harrington.

As everyone roamed around looking for a good seat, I stood and stared at the board of literary elements.

Literary Elements

SETTING	CHARACTERS	PLOT
Where?	Protagonist (+)	Events or Scenes
When?	Antagonist (-)	Conflict or Obstacles
	Main	(person vs. _____)
	Minor	Rising Action
	Changes	Climax
		Resolution

Man, she tricked me into reading. I just wanted to make sure I'd know what I was supposed to say.

"Do we get a grade?" Blythe asked, flipping through her notebook, half listening.

"Why does it matter, Blythe?" Mrs. Harrington raised her eyebrows.

"That way I know how much effort to put in." Blythe sat in a chair. "Those A's won't make themselves."

"You get A's?" José asked. "*Híjole! Wow!* I wonder what that feels like? *Justkidding.*"

"Anyway," Mrs. Harrington continued. "I thought we'd discuss the play and use the literary elements that I've written here on the board for you to use as we talk."

"Miss, what are the *Litter L, M, N, O, P's?*" It took me

a minute to figure out that José had mangled the words *literary elements*. What went on in that head of his?

"Look at the board, José." Mrs. Harrington pointed to her chart.

He squinted his eyes and turned his head to the side like a puppy who'd heard a weird noise.

"Only the literary elements or terms we've spent the last week copying down dictionary definitions for, and using in a sentence," Janie said.

"Oh, that! I remember *that*." El said. He pointed at Janie. "You are a *conflict*, Janie." See? José did actually know about literary elements. Why the act?

"Well, El," Janie responded. "You are an *antagonist* and an *obstacle*."

"What'd you call me?" José jerked his head.

"So, you can get points for asking questions or giving answers like Janie and José just did—sort of," Mrs. Harrington continued.

Silence.

"I'll start." Mrs. Harrington's eyes went up to the left. "For example, I could ask, "What's the *plot* of *A Christmas Carol*?"

"A *plot* is everything that happens on the soaps, Miss," Sophia offered, brushing her hair. She'd used all her makeup yesterday, so her beauty shop was temporarily shut down until she could get new supplies. "Like there's always a problem, like a chica who is trying to get your boyfriend."

"That's a *conflict*," Cliché said, shooting a look at Abhi, trying to show her she knew things, too.

"Right, it's the *problem*. Like I just said," Sophia clicked her tongue. "*Conflict* and *problem* are *cinnamons*."

"You mean SYNONYMS," Cliché said. "*Cinnamon* is what you put on your oatmeal."

"That's what I said!" Sophia replied, irritated. "So, anyways, you gotta push her back from your man and when she falls down, then everything is that *re*-thingy."

"*Resolved?*" Janie twisted up her face.

"Yeah, *that*," Sophia added. "What Janie said."

"I thought we were supposed to retell the plot of *A Christmas Carol* and not some silly soap!" Blythe scowled, and scribbled again in her notebook. Sophia put out her hand for Blythe to stop, and the blue-eye-shadow gang followed seconds later.

Mrs. Harrington wrote down a few things on her notepad and waited for someone to speak up. When no one said anything, she asked, "Who are the main characters of *A Christmas Carol*?"

"Characters? Is this a trick question?" José asked, holding up his index finger. "Because there's only *one,* Scrooge."

"But Scrooge is nothing without other characters," Abhi said. "There would be no plot—nothing would happen or change without the other characters. Scrooge would stay selfish."

"Points for Abhi and Scrooge—I mean José." Mrs. Harrington giggled.

"Ma'am, I think the Ghosts of Christmas Past, Present, and Future are also main characters," Janie said, "because they force Scrooge to look at how he acts in the world and how he could change himself and the world."

"Is that like an *obstacle* or problem, Mrs. Harrington?" Chewy asked.

"Points to you both." Mrs. Harrington smiled. "Good question, Janie. I want to piggyback on it. What do we call a character who works *against* the main character—or protagonist?"

"Mrs. Harrington," Blythe interrupted. "you still haven't said whether this is for a grade or not."

Everyone ignored Blythe.

Abhi said, "An *antagonist* is the character that works against the main character."

"I have a question, Mrs. Harrington." Blythe tapped the sides of her head with her fingers. "And it's a *thinker*, so really think about it." She glared at me. "What's the *smallest* part in the play?"

"Oh, I get it," Chewy said. "Tiny Tim is the *smallest* character because he's so tiny."

"Points for Blythe and . . . Chewy too, I guess . . ." Blythe faded off, recording her own points in the notebook, snapping it closed victoriously.

Mrs. Harrington glared at Blythe and wrote something in her notebook, too.

"What's the *climax*, or highest point in *A Christmas Carol*?"

"When Scrooge realizes Tiny Tim is going to die soon," Abhi said, "*if* he doesn't do something different."

"Die?" I said, "I never agreed to die." Though when

84

I thought about it, something as dramatic as a death could be fun to act out.

"Spoiler alert: Scrooge changes so you get live, TT," El explained.

How'd he know?

"My mom was so excited I got a part we logged into my sister's Webflix account and streamed the movie," El added. He pointed at me. "Hey everybody, let's call him TT from now on—or Tiny T?"

Blythe recorded it in her notebook, making it official.

"Tiny Tim is not a wrestler; he's a small, poor boy with a problem," Abhi said.

Yep, that's me, I thought: a small boy with a problem. That's my role. Here's a plot summary in the *Somebody/ Wanted/But/So* format Mrs. Harrington loved: I *wanted* to be Scrooge, *but* I'm Tiny Tim instead, *so* I wanted to crawl under a rock or at least skip rehearsal.

wwww

After English, lunch didn't even interest me. And it was Sloppy Joe day! But instead of hiding *under* a rock, I was a *on* a rock, exposed and roasting in the sunlight of embarrassment. The desert biome was my *setting.*

Points for me.

CHAPTER 17
YOU'RE TOAST!

In gym, after forcing us to do one hundred sit-ups, Coach O. had us walk laps while he talked with Mr. Akins under the basketball hoop. Flanked by Janie and Abhi, I tried not to complain. Mom says people don't want to listen to someone who complains all the time, so mostly I grumble in my head like a real Scrooge.

The three of us cringed when Blythe grabbed Mr. Akins's white bullhorn. *Screeeeeeeech!* "All theater students need to get to play practice."

Mr. Akins reached for his bullhorn, but Blythe kept moving it just out of his reach. "Miss Balboa!" His voice rose.

"Here you go. I'm finished with it now," Blythe said, handing it back to him. "Could you be a lamb and bring it by rehearsal?" Blythe tilted her head to the side, hands on hips. "Yeah, that'd be great."

Mr. Akins and Coach O. shrugged at each other in silence as we rushed to change back for rehearsal.

~~~

Later, in the cafetorium, Mrs. Darling instructed us on being actors and actresses. "The actor and actress must have a finely tuned body, showing feeling with his or her face, body, and voice." She pressed her hands into her lower back, looking like a bird of prey. "To that end, we will do specially designed exercises at the beginning of each rehearsal."

"Mrs. Darling," Chewy interrupted. "El Pollo Loco—I mean, José—isn't here yet."

"Where is José, anyway?" Marquis asked.

"I don't know," I said, and I didn't. Who knew with him?

"I'll find him." Blythe leapt from the wings to the front of the stage, then jumped to the floor like a cardigan ninja. She was out the door before Mrs. Darling could respond.

"But that's my . . ." Chewy muttered, tailing off and sinking into a chair behind Mrs. Darling.

"I want everyone on stage, lying flat on your backs, eyes closed." Mrs. Darling clapped out the syllables. "Pron-to!"

"You know what's funny, Mrs. Darling?" Marquis said. "It sounded like you said we should all lie down on the stage."

"She did," Abhi said. "And I bet we're closing our eyes for some visualization exercises."

"Well, I can see we have an experienced thespian in our mix," Mrs. Darling cooed.

With all of us lying around on the stage, it looked like a slumber party.

"Now everyone relax and lightly close your eyes." Mrs. Darling spoke slowly and calmly, as if she were hypnotizing us. "First, imagine you're a piece of crispy toast."

"Whole wheat or white?" Marquis asked, giggling.

"Pipe down!" Mrs. Darling snapped. "What you visualize is up to you. And from now on, I'll do all the talking, and you'll do all the silence. Toast doesn't *talKuh*." She hit the K in *talk* hard. "You are a piece of toast, fresh from the toaster, warm and crisp and brown. You're placed on a cool, white porcelain plate. Now imagine a cold butter knife spreading a pat of soft butter on you. Oh, yes. Feel it. Feel the butter on your warm crust."

Marquis and I jiggled like Jell-O, holding the laughs in.

"The melting butter tickles as it seeps into your nooks and crannies." Mrs. Darling ramped it up. "Now, *beeee* the toast. You are toast. What do you want?"

"I want some apricot jam," I whispered, and Marquis snorted and let loose, then Cliché, then Janie, then everyone.

The cafeteria doors flung open with a bang, and Blythe shoved El through the door in front of her.

The laughs stopped.

"I found him coming out of the boy's bathroom in the sixth-grade hall," Blythe announced. José's hands were tied behind his back with trash-bag twist ties.

"Miss," José whined. "It hurts. Make Sergeant Sweaters over here take this thing off of me."

"Blythe, what on earth have you done?" Mrs. Darling's sandals slapped the tile as she marched to them.

"You told me to apprehend the subject, and I had to improvise," Blythe said, like she was on a crime drama on Webflix. I wondered what he had done.

"You're not the PoPo!" El shouted. "She's out of control, Mrs. Darling."

"Chewy, get some scissors this instant," Mrs. Darling ordered.

"Chewy's not here," Blythe said, even though Chewy stood right there. "But I have some in my backpack."

Mrs. Darling turned José around. "Now, don't move a hair on your head." She sliced off the ties and they dropped to the floor.

José rubbed his wrists. "So, what'd I miss, Miss?"

"Are we still toast?" Cliché sat up. "Because if we are, some scrambled eggs would be nice."

"I missed snacks?" José leapt on stage and lay down between us. "I want some! Do you bring it around and drop in our mouths? I've never tried lying down to eat. That's *two* things I love. Snacks and naps." Boy, was he going to be disappointed when he figured out there were no snacks or naps.

After everyone settled flat on their backs again, Mrs. Darling whispered something to Blythe. But it was a stage whisper. Earlier, we'd learned that a stage whisper is when it sounds like you're whispering, but everyone can still hear you. "Listen, Missy, you have at least two strikes against you, probably much more, but I am warning you now, you'll be out of the Actin' Alamos if you woman-handle anyone else. Is that clear?" Mrs. Darling waited, palm up.

Blythe handed over the rest of her zip ties. "Yes, ma'am. Duly noted." Blythe returned to her dark lair in the wings of the stage.

"I'll dispose of those for you, Mrs. Darling," Chewy said.

"Thank you, dear man."

Blushing, Chewy slipped the leftover ties in the front pocket of his khakis.

"Miss, when do I get *my* toast?" El asked. "I'll take the heel since I was late."

"Tomorrow, be here on time and perhaps you'll get to be something even better," she replied sharply, like a knife slicing toast in half. "Silence!"

"This time, I want you to picture snow in your mind's eye."

"But it doesn't snow in San Antonio!" El sat up.

"Lie down, El." Mrs. Darling's floaty, whispery voice became annoyed. "IMAGINE! You've seen snow in movies." I couldn't see her, but I *imagined* she was rubbing her temples. I heard her take three deep breaths. "Breathe in, breathe out, breathe in." We realized she was talking to us, so we breathed in . . . and out.

I relaxed and visualized white snow, tiny floating white cotton balls.

"And now," Mrs. Darling's smooth voice floated above the stage again, "you are a snowflake."

We breathed in and out.

"Now, take your time to stand please," Mrs. Darling said as if she were the sky itself.

We rose from the stage, her willing snow zombies. All that breathing had calmed me. And now I was a floaty cotton ball, soft and round.

"The wind is picking up and beginning to blow you around, snowflakes."

Slowly, we stood and swayed with the imaginary wind.

"The wind is blowing you to the right," she said, and under her spell, we floated right.

"Wait!" Mrs. Darling called out. "Another gust is taking you near the edge of the stage, then it throws you back."

And we moved up and then quickly back, following her every direction.

"Now, you're spinning. You're caught up in the wind, moving freely on your own wind now. Move!" Mrs. Darling, Queen of the Sky, commanded. "Flail about, snowflakes. Go as you may!"

We spun. We flailed. Arms lifted higher and higher, El spun faster and faster.

"Good, El," Mrs. Darling commented. "Your arms are loosey-goosey and free."

Blythe stood in the wings, observing and taking notes.

"Watch El!" Mrs. Darling cheered.

And we stopped for a moment and watched.

"There's my lead! Floppsy woppsy! Droppsy loppsy! My little snowflake, you are free!" Mrs. Darling smiled.

It almost looked like José actually got caught up in a gust of wind. Moving in front of everybody seems so easy for him. It's hard for me to relax and just be silly. I was jealous of that.

"Rejoin! Rejoice!" Mrs. Darling sang: "We are no longer people on a stage. No, we are snow on the wind. Be free, all ye snowflakes!" It was getting weird, but then we joined in—spinning, blowing, floating—like we were real snowflakes.

And I felt loosey-goosey too. I laughed and my eyes met Abhi's and Janie's and even El's.

And José spun faster and faster and even faster. I don't know if he was making up for being late, or if he was up to his old tricks. But el Copo de Nieve Loco—the crazy snowflake—moved like a blur.

"Be like El. Be free, my snowflakes." Mrs. Darling's voice verged on tears.

El's hands went up higher and higher, until—smack!— his floppsy hand slapped Chewy's face.

"Ow!" Clewy squawked. "That hurt!"

"Everyone freeze!" Mrs. Darling yelled in that low you-better-do-it-or-else voice.

We froze.

"Get it?" said José. "We're *snow*, and she told us to *freeze?*"

Nobody laughed.

We all surrounded Chewy, who rubbed his cheek while Mrs. Darling checked on him.

"Are you okay, m'dear?" Mrs. Darling gently looked at his cheek like Chewy was a wounded toddler.

"I guess," Chewy snapped, pointing at José. "But you better keep your hands to yourself!"

Mrs. Darling hugged him. *"Shhhhhh!"*

"Do you want me to open an incident report, ma'am?"

Blythe circled, tapping her notebook in her hand like a police baton.

"YOU, go to the office and get a bag of ice," Mrs. Darling pointed her green nail at Blythe. "And YOU." She pointed right at José.

José shrugged and looked behind himself. "Who, me?"

"Oh, yes, YOU, Mr. Soto, my actor extraordinaire. You must know I absolutely adore your passion, your free soul, but my dear, you must learn the art of restraint."

"These twist ties are restraints." Chewy pulled the confiscated twist ties from his khakis. He stared at José.

"Not literal restraints like that, Chewy," Mrs. Darling clarified.

Chewy crossed his arms, pouting.

"*Restraint* means holding back some, so you don't leave damage in your wake."

"Or slapped faces," Chewy mumbled, staring at José and not blinking.

"José, dear," Mrs. Darling explained, "one can't hurt others with art. Art makes us think—not say *ouch*. Actin' Alamos keep their hands to themselves. Freedom doesn't mean losing control. Now, you must apologize to Chewy and hold back just a tetch."

"Sorry, *sorry*, sorry," José said.

Mrs. Darling bellowed, "Everybody, take ten!"

CHAPTER 18
THE READ-THROUGH

The ten-minute break allowed me time to share a string cheese with Abhi. I wasn't at home alone, talking to the cabinets. I was living.

"Now let's get down to the read-through," Mrs. Darling demanded, all business. "A read-through is when you just read the play aloud, but you don't move around." It sounded like reader's theater in fifth grade.

Blythe stomped out from the wings and scribbled something in her notebook, then stepped back into her stage wing.

"Let's begin," Mrs. Darling said.

As Scrooge, José had the first line of the play. He read aloud: "(*Scrooge enters stage left, into a spare office, wearing wire-rimmed glasses on the end of his nose*)."

"Darling, we don't read the stage directions," Mrs.

Darling explained, looking over her lime-green half-glasses.

"You *do* the stage directions during the play; you don't *read* them!" Janie shook her head, irritated.

"I can read the stage directions, Director Darling." Blythe stepped out of the darkness again.

Chewy growled.

Mrs. Darling sighed. "You know, Blythe, you *could* read those over." From her tone, you could tell Mrs. Darling had had just about enough. "The light is better in the hallway, so we'll see you in a bit." She motioned toward the door. "Go along, dear. That way we won't disturb you by reading our lines."

Chewy smiled.

Holding her open script, Blythe nodded slowly as she backed out of the cafetorium, watching us closely, as if she were committing this whole event to memory for a later report.

Mrs. Darling waited for Blythe to shut the door. "Action!" Mrs. Darling yelled.

"Action," Chewy whispered, holding the side of his face.

José actually read only his lines this time: "So, I see from your shivering you think it's *too* cold in here, Cratchit? I bet you think we should throw some coal from my coal box on the fire. Well, think again, unless you want to find another job. (*Nephew enters stage left, striding cheerfully.*)"

"You're reading the stage direction again!" Chewy griped.

Janie quietly banged her forehead on the cafetorium table.

"But it's right after my lines," José grumbled. "How am I supposed to know the difference? I'm not a playwright. I'm just your average handsome star, doing his best to charm audiences, young and old."

Mrs. Darling sighed, and tossed her script on a table. Chewy did the same thing. "I wrote the stage directions in *italics* and put them between *parentheses*!" She arched her hands into huge parentheses, framing her reddening face.

"What'd you call me?" José slapped his thigh, looking around for others to join in laughing. They didn't. "*Justkidding.*"

"Next scene!" Mrs. Darling was done talking.

"Cliché, you'll read the nephew this round," Mrs. Darling directed, "but we'll make you a niece."

Blythe's head pressed against the glass on the cafetorium door, trying to listen.

"Cliché, would you be so kind as to read the next line?"

"Hello, Uncle. Merry Christmas," Cliché read stiffly.

"Bah. Humbug." El Pollo Loco read flatly.

"Humbug to Christmas, Uncle?" Cliché read.

"José! José!" Mrs. Darling interrupted. "Use your feelings and experiences and channel them into your role. Think about your deep disappointment at missing my toast exercise. Use those real feelings of frustration for the raw emotion you showed us in the auditions."

"Bah! Humbug!" El screamed. His restraint was short-lived.

"Yes!" Mrs. Darling's eyes closed. "YES!"

"Bah! HUMMMbug!" El shouted louder.

"Again!" Ecstatic, Mrs. Darling rocked her head from side to side, lost in José's humbugging.

"Mrs. Darling." Janie tapped the nonexistent watch on her wrist. "If we don't pick up the pace, we'll never get to the part with the ghosstsss."

"That's my j—" Chewy began.

The cafeteria doors burst open. "Bah! Humbug!" Blythe yelled, coming in from the hall. "The stage manager will get us ALL back on track."

And somehow after that, we read through the script without any more trouble—or stage directions. Since Mrs. Darling's adaptation was so short, we got to the ghosts and, to my disappointment, to Tiny Tim. Mrs. Darling really does know how to write, though. There were all kinds of words, and they were all spelled right. She only left off one closing parenthesis on stage directions, and Blythe pointed it out. She double-checked each script to ensure the correction was made.

At the end of rehearsal, Blythe, still trying to direct things, offered, "I think *I* deserve EXTRA extra credit in Mrs. Harrington's class for finding your mistake!"

Chewy looked devastated.

Mrs. Darling didn't respond.

CHAPTER 19
REHEARSING GRATITUDE

At rehearsal the next day, Mrs. Darling started blocking the play. Blocking was like a GPS for the stage, pinning your location on a map, except the map was the stage and your location was where you stood to say your lines. And you had to "hit" certain "marks" at certain times. It's like memorizing lines, but it's memorizing movement instead. As alternate, I was supposed to take notes on everybody's movement, which was a little more than I could get done. The only person who had it all written down was Blythe. She must go through several pencils a day.

Mrs. Darling had insisted we learn our lines quickly, so we could be "off book" by next Monday. *Off book* means you've memorized your lines (*and* stage directions).

It didn't seem like José was taking learning his lines—

or blocking—seriously, but he sure was enthusiastic about the acting part. On Tuesday and Wednesday, he was late to practice again though. Blythe thought it was because she wasn't allowed to hunt down and woman-handle him or any other late kids. Something about a fear of a lawsuit.

Anyway, because José wasn't there, I had to read his lines and mine. Day after day, I was the guy who showed up on time. The guy who did all the work, and I knew José would be the one who'd get all the adoration of the audience when we performed the play. Nobody sees rehearsals. They just see the show. What on earth was he doing?

Once he arrived, he sneaked a chug of Mrs. Darling's soda. She almost caught him once because he smeared some of her lipstick on his lip from the can, and he also burped all his lines. But line burping didn't make Mrs. Darling furious like "stepping on lines" did. Mrs. Darling explained that stepping on lines is when you speak over the other person's line before they're finished. Kind of like not waiting your turn, so you can see how that'd be a problem for one Pollo Loco.

ᴡᴡᴡᴡ

Thursday's rehearsal began differently—José was on time.

"Remember how yesterday, we visualized you were my can of soda—fizzing and tingling our noses?" Mrs. Darling said. "Well, today we're going to use discussion with a partner to study a time in our past when we had a similar emotion to the one our character has in *A Christmas Carol*."

"This is fun!" Janie rubbed her hands together.

"Indeed!" Mrs. Darling said. "Work with a partner when you're not onstage today. Okay, Marquis and José to the stage. The rest of you explore your character's feelings."

I sat thinking about how Tiny Tim felt. He was so happy, but he didn't have any reason to be as far as I could see. So, I thought of a time I felt happiness. The first thing that popped in my head was from a few days ago when Abhi asked me to sit next to her on the bus.

Thinking about how I felt then, I rose up from my chair and walked over to Abhi, who sat at a table by herself. "Will you run lines with me, Abs?" I was playing the role of someone confident and normal.

"I'd love to." Abhi stood up. "But don't call me Abs. It reminds me of doing 100 sit-ups for Coach O. this week."

We giggled and placed our hands on our own tummies at the same exact time. "Yeah, it still hurts to laugh!" Abhi said.

While Mrs. Darling worked on a scene with Mr. Cratchit and Ebenezer, Abhi and I sat at a table in the back of the cafetorium.

"Why don't we try Mrs. Darling's exercise?" Abhi prompted.

"Okay," I said, glad to extend my time with the most interesting girl I'd ever known. "Who goes first?"

"I choose you," Abhi said. I tried to act like my face wasn't flushing red, but the ends of her lips curled up.

"I'm not sure what to do." I looked at a cobweb in the corner.

"Oh, I can go first if it helps," Abhi said. "So, I am

Mrs. Cratchit," Abhi said, "and I'm worried about my family having enough to eat."

"Yeah," I said. "I get hungry a lot."

"But I think Mrs. Cratchit feels like she needs to protect her family. It's like my cat Smokey. When a dog starts running at him, I want to hold him close and protect him. I could use that feeling of worry to help me play a protective Mrs. Cratchit."

Stunned, I stared at her in silence. She was so smart and kind and pretty.

"So, Zack, think of a time in your life when you were in a situation like Tiny Tim," Abhi prompted me.

"I've never been on crutches." I squinted.

"Think of time you had something hard to deal with, and you were strong and happy in spite of it, like Tiny Tim."

"I guess when I'm Tiny Tim," I said, "my heart is supposed to be full of love, no matter what's happening in my life."

Abhi nodded.

"And like, this dude is on crutches and could die soon and is hungry and poor and all he wants is to live his life and enjoy it." As I said it, I realized Tiny Tim never complains about the role he's been given in life.

"This is good, Zack."

Then it came to me: "Tiny Tim just feels joy and gratitude for what he *does* have."

"I think you've got it, Zack." Abhi smiled.

"So maybe I could use that I didn't get the role I wanted as my thing to not complain about. And be happy for what

I do have." I paused. "Like now."

This time her teeth showed when she smiled.

"Looks like the scene is over, and we're going on to a new one," Abhi said, looking at the stage, changing the subject.

"Yep," I nodded. "It sure does." And I wasn't disappointed. No. I was grateful for the time I did have. With Abhi.

As we floated back to join the others, I thought about the role I'd been playing. I'd been kind of a Scrooge, not appreciating that I did have a role. I was *in* the play. I wasn't alone at home, watching *Judge Joe*. I was part of things. I decided I was going to be more like Tiny Tim and stop complaining.

That night, I called Marquis and told him all about my sesh with Abhi and he told me about his with Cliché. She really wanted to be Mrs. Cratchit.

"Everybody wants to be married to the Marquis." Marquis giggled.

I did, too.

It felt good to laugh with my best friend. Maybe this play was going to be fun after all.

CHAPTER 20

THE PUPPET MASTER

On Friday in English, Mrs. Harrington asked, "How's the play going?"

Chewy let loose. "*Some* people don't show up to practice on time or learn their lines. And as Cliché says, 'When the cat is away'"—Chewy motioned his head at Blythe—"'the mouse will play.'"

"*Hissssss!*" El made clawing motions at Chewy.

Janie shook her head. "No, El, in this scenario *you're* the *mouse*, and Blythe is the cat."

El turned and hissed at Blythe and Chewy, wildly clawing the air like the naughty kitty he was.

Chewy rolled his eyes.

Janie smacked her forehead.

"Well, that's what happens when there's an absence of leadership, ma'am," Blythe mumbled, uncharacteristically without a cardigan. Her hair was pressed flat in the back like she'd slept on it, and it looked like it could use a washing and a brushing. Her skin had a grayish tint. I guess the stress of being stage manager was getting to her.

"Are you okay, Blythe?" Mrs. Harrington asked, truly concerned.

"Is a battery-operated toy okay when you take away its battery?" Since Blythe had been stripped of her theater cop duties, she stayed in the unlit wings on the side of the stage, eating animal crackers from an enormous plastic tub from Costco. Blythe shaded her eyes with her hands. "Why is it so bright in here?"

"Miss, she's just mad because she's not allowed to detain or cuff us anymore," José said.

"What?" Mrs. Harrington asked, confused.

"I *only* did what was necessary," Blythe said, staring out the window, wistfully.

"But it was *my* job," Chewy argued.

"Was it?" Blythe turned her head. "Is it? When will you actually *do* something?"

Mrs. Harrington's face twisted up.

"Well, Chewy." Blythe dug deep and found the last of her bossy voice again, bossy as ever. "I suggest you get this cast under control because when I pull up that curtain next Friday, it doesn't come down till the very end." She stood and mic-dropped her notebook.

Chewy scrambled to grab the notebook, but Blythe slammed her foot down on it like it was a cockroach in her kitchen. Blythe says she wants to be a principal when she grows up, so she can get everybody to act right. But Mrs.

Darling had forced Blythe to hang up her cardigan and turn in her twist ties. She was powerless.

"Chewy! DO YOUR JOB!" Blythe screamed, rubbing her cardiganless arms. "My hands are tied. YOU have to be the one. Destiny is calling!"

"But I don't have a phone." Chewy was frustrated. "And who's this Destiny, and why is she calling me?"

"Well," José said, "I'm glad your hands are tied now and mine aren't. Hey, Mrs. H., I got to go to the little boy's room."

As José walked out the door, Blythe stomped over to Chewy and whispered something in his ear.

Chewy nodded, got up, and followed El to the bathroom.

~~~~~

Later that day in rehearsal, Mrs. Gage shuffled in with a note. Mrs. Darling stopped and read it. "Right now?"

"It's a disciplinary referral," Mrs. Gage said. "Mr. Akins wants to see him immediately."

"José, you need to gather your things and go with Mrs. Gage," Mrs. Darling said flatly.

José had been on time again today, so it didn't make sense. He'd been coming on time; he knew his lines and his blocking. What now?

Chewy stared nervously at the ground. Blythe glanced over in Chewy's direction, giving him two thumbs up. She wore her cardigan again and had brushed her hair.

After José walked out of the cafetorium, a hush swallowed up the cast.

"Does anybody have any idea of what happened?" Mrs. Darling eyed all of us.

"Um, well . . ." Chewy's eyes darted to Blythe, and she nodded the go-ahead. "Did anybody notice Manny the custodian mopping up the water in the sixth-grade hall?"

"Yes, I had to hold my sheets up to keep them dry," Janie answered.

"What's that got to do with José?" Cliché asked.

"Let the boy speak!" Blythe snapped.

"I got this!" Chewy yelled.

Blythe flinched.

"As I was saying," Chewy continued. "A toilet-clogging incident occurred in the boys' restroom, ma'am." Chewy spoke in an authoritative voice. At that moment, I realized Blythe wasn't playing her role anymore; Chewy was. I guess when someone moves out of one role, someone else takes it over.

"Oh, my!" Mrs. Darling said, collapsing into a chair. "This is not good."

"He tried to clog the toilet with handfuls of toilet paper. I saw him." Now Chewy couldn't stop. "You don't mess with the Fightin' Alamos' toilets, ma'am." Chewy tapped his pencil on his clipboard. "Nope. They are quite essential to a healthy school environment."

Who *was* this guy?

"You're brave," Janie said. "It's not always easy to stand up and do the right thing, Chewy."

"Ha! If puppets are brave," Cliché said. "It's obvious who's pulling Chewy's strings."

Abhi's eyes teared up.

Chewy looked at his sleeve for a loose string, but everyone else figured it out at once. Blythe had put Chewy up to catching José doing whatever he does when he's in the boy's bathroom—Blythe, the puppet master.

Janie looked right at Blythe. "You weren't going to be satisfied till you ridded this play of . . . one . . . of its most enthusiastic actors."

"He was trouble, Janie," Chewy said.

Everybody had a role, I guess. Chewy was the enforcer now. But what was my role in all of this? I was mad that José getting in trouble made Abhi sad. I mean, I know I was playing Tiny Tim, and I was an alternate. But who was Zack Delacruz in life, really?

I've stood up to El Pollo Loco before. But now Chewy had stood up to him, too. That must've been why he followed José to the restroom during English. He witnessed the vandalism and filled out an incident report on José. That took Blythe-like guts, and I guess we all take on other roles when needed. I guess if El Pollo Loco did something wrong, he should get in trouble. Was that his role? The one who got in trouble?

I collapsed in my chair and looked at Abhi, who shook her head no.

What started as a rehearsal ended as a reversal.

Not too long after José was escorted to the office, he returned. His eyes were bloodshot, and for the first time ever, he didn't utter a sound. He handed Mrs. Darling a note and left.

When the door shut, Mrs. Darling read the note. "Well, it seems the school discipline panel has decided"— Mrs. Darling looked up from the paper—"José Soto will be suspended for three days and will not be allowed to participate in extracurricular activities for the rest of the semester."

"Does that mean he can't be in the play?" Abhi asked Mrs. Darling.

"I'm afraid so, dear," Mrs. Darling replied, the ends of her lips curling down.

"NOOOOO!" We reacted to the news.

"Are we going to have to cancel the play?" Marquis zipped his powder-blue warm-up down and up, down and up.

"That'd be the end of the world." Cliché looked at Marquis.

"No," Abhi replied, sounding stronger. "That's why we have alternates. El would want the show to go on."

"You mean I have to be Scrooge?" Cliché asked.

"Or Zack," Abhi said, trying to smile.

"Zack, you'll have to be the new Scrooge," Mrs. Darling announced. "And Cliché you'll be Tiny Tim."

What? I thought. I felt punched in the gut. But I didn't want to be Scrooge anymore. I wanted to be grateful for what I had. I had memorized Tiny Tim's lines already, anyway. I finally wanted to be Tiny Tim. Plus, to tell the truth, José was really good at the acting part. I didn't want it take from him. And I didn't know if I could be as good as he was. But I didn't say a word.

"Good job!" Marquis patted me on the shoulder.

"Job?" I stiffened. "I didn't *do* anything."

"All good things to those who wait!" Janie quoted. "Disney's *Tangled*, two thousand ten, starring Broadway darling Donna Murphy as the wise Mother Gothel."

But I wasn't so sure it *was* a good thing anymore.

"I miss El already." Abhi sighed.

"Yes, Zack, you have big shoes to fill," Mrs. Darling said.

"Yeah," Marquis nodded. "José would've made a joke about your tiny feet now, Zack."

"*Justkidding,*" we all said once. Even Mrs. Darling. Even me. But not Blythe. *And not Chewy.*

At that moment, I didn't remember ever wanting to play Scrooge at all. I didn't know what to think or say or do. Luckily, Cliché had plenty to say.

"Um, reality check, Mrs. Darling. Tiny Tim is a boy and I'm a girl, so—"

"Actually, Cliché, in the thea-TUH there is a long tradition of male actors playing female roles," Mrs. Darling shot back.

"But that was because women weren't allowed to!" Janie said.

"Exactly my point, Janie." Mrs. Darling was on a roll. "Now the women can play men. It's reversed. I'm giving women *more* opportunities, not *fewer.*"

"Oh, yeah," Janie agreed. "Good point. Looks like Mother Gothel isn't the only wise *older* woman."

"*Humph!*" Mrs. Darling said. "Places everyone!"

I never really thought about *male* and *female* as a role we play.

"So," Cliché begged, "can I at least change the name to Tiny Tina?"

"I should hope not," Janie threw back the layers of ghost sheets, which dropped to the ground in a heap. "There's no need to change the name. You're an actress. Act. ACT, I say!" Janie raised her fist.

Cliché crossed her arms, smirking.

"Yes," Abhi sighed. "El showed us how we all could act more."

"You'll be my son," Marquis said to Cliché. And that's

all it took to change Cliché from peeved to pleased.

"You're my son, too," Abhi said.

Cliché turned away from Abhi, rolling her eyes. Well, she looked less peeved, anyway.

I wasn't smiling either. I was worrying. I was worrying about José. As crazy as he was, he was kind of a friend. Man, he looked sad, and he was really into the acting thing. It seemed like Blythe was on the warpath. Who'd be next? Would there be anybody left? Worries flooded my mind.

But it all hit me at once: I had a new role to play besides worrier. "You mean I've got to learn all the lines by the end of next week?"

"Yes, but remember," Mrs. Darling reassured me, "it's an abbreviated version, so it's not that much at all to learn really."

"But is there like one minute of the whole play when Scrooge isn't onstage?"

Wait. Was I complaining?

"I know, Zack! Isn't it divine?" Mrs. Darling beamed. "You'll shine in front of everybody for almost the entire play! What a role to play!"

Wait! Now I was Scrooge. Was I supposed to complain?

"You'll be great." Abhi patted me on the shoulder, not yet smiling, but being brave, even though I know she's one of José's friends. "Congratulations."

I mean, José got on my nerves, but he was a great Scrooge.

So that afternoon, with one-fourth of my confidence, I read my new part of Ebenezer Scrooge. I hadn't even had the chance to highlight my new lines, but everybody was patient with me. And kind. I walked my blocking and hit my marks. Mostly. In between my lines, when I should have been listening to the other characters, I was thinking about what Mom always said: "Be careful what you wish for—you just might get it." I got it, and I get it.

Get it?

Got it.

Good.

When I looked at Abhi watching me from a chair in the audience, I got a knot in my stomach. Not the gurgle one, but the one that feels like you're hungry and you need to eat something small except you're almost queasy, so you wait.

I winked at her.

She smiled and looked down at her script.

My confidence charge went from 25 percent to 50 percent. That's right, Mr. G. I converted fascinating fractions to perfect percentages—like a boss.

"**A** lead role is worth celebrating." Mom had picked me up after practice to start our weekend early. Dad had a date that night. Don't ask. Mom said we'd have our own date. She took me out to her favorite restaurant, La Fonda. I loved their enchiladas verdes.

In the Honda on the way over, Mom was Mom. She threw question balls at me and I wanted to dodge them. I wasn't in the mood. "So why did José have to drop out of the play?"

"I don't know."

"You don't know?"

"God, Mom! It was a urinal-related incident."

Mom let out a loud laugh. Luckily, Mom wasn't drinking coffee like she does when she drives me to school in the mornings. She definitely would have spit it out on the dashboard. "I'm afraid to ask for more details."

"I'm afraid to give them to you." I adjusted in my seat. "Let's just say he likes to *potty* like there's no tomorrow."

"So, he's a *potty* animal?" Mom snorted a laugh. This was the most fun we'd had in a while. "Okay. Let's change the subject."

There's Mom again, I thought. But it was fun while it lasted. To tell the truth, I really had been bothered by the whole restroom-at-school thing. At the auditions, I had to go to the bathroom, and I couldn't. I just couldn't.

"We can change the subject, but only a little." I took a deep breath and asked a question I really wanted the answer to. "Did you ever go number two at school?"

"Stop it, Zack," Mom said. She didn't think I was serious.

"No, Mom," I said slowly and calmly. "I'm serious."

"Are you?" She side-eyed me.

"Yes. I swear." I nodded my head.

Mom took a deep breath. "Okay. Yes, I did, but I didn't like to."

"Why?" I asked.

"I don't know." Mom shrugged. "I guess it just seems like such a private thing."

"Because of the noises?" I asked.

"That's a nice way to put it, Zack." Mom cleared her throat. "Yes, I'd say the noises were part of my hesitance."

"And the smells," I added. "And there's never any toilet paper."

"No," Mom said, "We had toilet paper in the girls' room."

"Well." I shook my head and looked out the passenger window. "We don't in the boys'."

"How do you know there isn't toilet paper?"

"Because I do need something to blow my nose on."

"Why are you asking about this, Zack?"

"I haven't ever gone number two at school before," I said. "And the other day I really needed to, but I couldn't do it."

Mom looked over at me for a second. "Do you still get a nervous tummy?"

"Sometimes."

"I'm glad you asked, Zack." Mom turned the wheel into the parking lot of La Fonda.

We stayed in the car after Mom shut off the ignition.

"In between classes, the restroom is like a zoo."

"So," Mom offered, "get a pass and go during class."

I nodded, but that's not as easy as it sounds. Teachers think you want to go to the bathroom to goof off. And I guess José *did* go to the bathroom to goof off.

"You know, Zack," Mom said, and handed me a packet of tissue.

"I'm not crying, Mom," I said.

"I know, Zack." Mom patted my left knee. "Keep that in your pocket on nervous tummy days. And let me know when you need more."

I looked at the triple-ply, super-absorbent personal care wipes. "Thanks, Mom."

"Shall we?"

wwww

"I've got a lot of lines to learn." I walked up the red steps to the restaurant fast, so I could hold open the heavy wooden door for Mom.

"Thank you." Mom walked past me. "I can help you with lines. I did that when I was in a drama club in high school."

"Wait," I said. "*You* were in a play?"

"Don't look so shocked, Zack," Mom said. "I had a life before you."

The hostess led us to a table for two in the cool evening air. Leaves rustled in the breeze, sounding like a deck of cards being shuffled.

I guess I'd never really thought about Mom as a teenager. I hope she didn't wear that gold real-estate jacket when she was in high school, or hand out her business cards to everyone she met.

"What a nice night." Mom took in a long breath.

After we sat at our table, I kept going. "How come you never said you were in a play?" I looked at Mom dipping a tortilla chip in a bowl of red salsa.

"You never asked." She crunched a tortilla chip.

"Were you the lead?" I took a long gulp of iced water.

"As a matter of fact"—Mom sipped her iced tea—"I was one of them. I was Ms. Barrett, the English teacher, in *Up the Down Staircase*."

"*Up the Down Staircase*?" I asked. "That doesn't make any sense."

"That was sort of the point, I think." Mom leaned forward. "It was about a boy who broke all the rules, like going up the DOWN staircase."

"Like José?"

"I suppose so," Mom agreed. "But older. And no urinal stuff that I remember." She got all happy-looking. "I played this young teacher, who tried to reach the tough guy and make him feel like he could be successful."

"So, sort of like a young Mrs. Darling."

"Yeah." Mom nodded and crunched.

We just sat there and talked like the only thing that mattered was the two of us. It used to feel like this with the three of us—Mom, Dad, and me. But now I have to have a different way to be with each of them. We still play our roles, but we're not all in the same scenes anymore.

"How'd you learn all your lines?" I asked.

"I read them a bunch of times, but whenever I had a monologue—"

"What's that?" I asked.

"It's a big chunk to say all at once."

I nodded.

"So when I had a monologue," Mom explained, "I'd read it into a tape recorder two or three times, and then play it over and over as I was falling asleep, play it while I brushed my teeth and got ready for school. I even listened to it on my Walkman on my way to school."

"What's a Walkman?"

"When I was a kid, a Walkman was a tape player you could carry with you."

"What's a tape player?"

Mom sighed. "Like a huge cell phone."

"Could you play games on it?" I asked.

"No."

"Could you call people on it?" I cut a piece of my cheese enchilada with my fork and took a bite while I waited for my answer.

"Well, no."

"What could you do on it?" I asked.

"You could play a tape." Mom dabbed the side of her mouth. "That was it."

"What's a tape?"

"They were how you played songs."

"*Wooow*! Why didn't you just use your cell phone?"

"*Because they weren't invented yet.*"

"I'm glad I wasn't a kid when you were," I said, then took a sip through my straw.

"That makes two of us!"

I laughed—not knowing what she meant—and finished off my ice water.

"I suppose we could get *you* a cell phone." Mom put down her drink. "Since it's for school."

"Whaaaat?"

"An early Christmas present. I already talked to your Dad about it. You'll just get it early."

I couldn't believe it. "I didn't know you talked to Dad when I'm not there. I mean, I guess I did."

"We're not married anymore." Mom put down her fork. "But we're still your mom and dad. And we think you're ready."

"That's awesome!"

"But if you break it or lose it, we're not replacing it, so take care of it."

A cell phone that records, so I can practice my lines for

118

the part I wanted! And I get my Christmas present early. I guess that's what they mean by a Christmas miracle.

I ate the rest of my enchiladas so fast that I had to wait on mom to finish her tostada. I swore she was eating slowly just to pull my chain.

wwm

On the way home, we stopped at the Grasshopper Wireless store. A real nice lady named Denise showed me how I could record on a voice memo app. My mom was impressed. Denise set it all up for me. It's not only a voice memo recorder, it's also a camera, a music player, and—oh, yeah—a phone. With this kind of phone, I felt like a seventh- or eighth-grader. And I knew who I wanted to call. But who would get my first call ever on my first phone ever?

I had to choose.

Abhi or Marquis?

I knew what I had to do first.

Marquis's phone rang and rang and rang.

No answer. I patiently waited five full minutes (yes, I watched the clock on Mom's microwave, so I'm sure).

I called again and just kept letting it ring. His grandmother, Ma, doesn't believe in voice mail, so it will ring and ring until I hang up. Mom tried to say eight rings is a polite number, but I couldn't think of any reason someone wouldn't pick up their phone. I had news. I had my first phone.

Finally, Marquis's grandmother, Ma, picked up. "Lord, have mercy! This better not be a sales call! Because we certainly don't want whatever you're selling."

"No, Ma," I said. "It's me, Zack. I'm not selling anything."

"Zack, you all right?" Ma asked. "You were about to wear my phone ringer plum out."

"Sorry, I just got a phone, and I wanted Marquis to be my first call," I explained.

"Glory be," Ma said. "Your very own phone. *Mmm-mmm.* One thing you gotta know is it's polite to let the phone ring only eight times."

What was the deal with adults and eight rings?

"But it kept ringing and ringing and . . ." Ma sighed. "Well, I'm glad you're okay, but I know you didn't call to talk to me."

After I told Marquis I got the phone, he started calling me Phone Man.

"So, Phone Man," Marquis said. "Are you saying we can call Cliché and Abhi whenever we want?"

"Yep, we can do almost anything now!" I lay on my bed on top of my bedspread on my phone, like a baller. "We can jam out, or I can record my lines . . ."

"What do you mean *record your lines*?"

"Mom said I could read my Scrooge lines into a voice memo and then play them while I lie here, or on the bus, or anytime with my earbuds."

"Phone Man," Marquis asked, "are you telling me your phone came with earbuds?"

"I am."

"And you're the star of the play."

"Don't remind me."

"Too late, Phone Man!"

Tap. Tap. Mom knocked on my door.

So, I'm a baller with a mother. That's how I roll.

121

"Mom's knocking on my door, so I better go." I sat up on the edge of my bed.

"Don't you have some lines to record anyway?" Marquis poked fun at me.

"You'll see." I stood and walked over to the door. "My plan will work. I'll get these lines down in no time."

I ended my call and opened the door. "What?"

I guess it sounded a little snappy because she said, "That doesn't sound like someone who just got a new phone." Mom folded her arms.

"Sorry, Mom." I took a breath and looked her in the eye. "Thanks so much, Mom. This is the coolest thing ever. I was just calling Marquis."

"I'm glad you like it." Mom gave me a hug.

"Well, don't stay up learning your lines too long, all right?" Mom held me in the hug till I replied.

"Yes, ma'am."

"I love you, Zack."

"I love you, too, Mom."

I shut my door. I didn't need to be tucked in anymore. But I could almost feel her cheek resting against my door. Don't parents have anything else to do than worry about what their kids are doing all the time? Glory B! What does that even mean? "Glory B," I repeated it as I searched "Glory B" on my phone to see what it means. I was a man now. And I had a phone. By the way, it's "Glory be," as in "Glory be to the Father." Thanks, Internet! I guess they're called smartphones because they make you smarter.

I got out my copy of the *Christmas Carol* script and opened it to the first page. I spoke into my phone, and immediately recorded my first scene. I stopped and listened to it. I was kind of shocked. My voice didn't sound the way it sounded in my head. I recorded another scene, and I listened over and over and over until I fell asleep. I slept Scrooge. I woke up Scrooge. And rode the bus Scrooge (with my earbuds, of course).

And that's how it went the rest of the week at Mom's. I learned a lot of my lines.

Dad was excited to see my phone when I got to his house Sunday night. I had called him on it a few times, but he hadn't seen it. I know it was just a phone, but my mom reminded that me half of it was from him. We stayed up a little too late talking. I had missed Dad. And as cool as a phone is, there's nothing like talking in person.

Especially when it's to your mom or dad.

CHAPTER 24
THE OLD BALL AND CHAIN

When Marquis and I arrived at the cafeteria for breakfast, there was more good news.

"Hey, Phone Man!" Marquis elbowed me. "Pancakes!"

We stood and breathed in the sweet smell of syrup that filled the room. Marquis looked over. "If you look up the word origin of *pancakes* on your phone, you're on your own."

Marquis and I devoured the steamed miniature blueberry pancakes out of the clear plastic bags they were served in. You only got one ladle of syrup in a little white paper cup, so we tried to conserve our syrup by spacing out our pancake dips. There'd be no extra syrup. We didn't even try it; we knew Mrs. O'Shansky would give a lecture and make you feel dumb in front of the whole line.

The news of the week pinged around in my head. Being back at Dad's apartment was great because it meant I was riding the bus with Marquis again. This was also the bad news: My fantasy of running lines on the bus with Abhi had come to an end. And the terrifying and terrific news: The play is this Friday. I never noticed how the words *terrific* and *terrifying* are so close.

"Marquis, you're going to want to hear this," I said, perching my phone in front of me, ready to read.

"Did you find something else on that know-it-all phone to phonesplain to me?" Marquis grinned.

I smirked back. "Very funny. But think about the words *terror* and *terrible*. Both have negative connotations, right?"

"Zack, Mrs. Harrington would be so proud you used *connotation* when the one syllable word *tone* would have sufficed." Marquis laughed. "It's nice to know that you are using the time you've been ignoring me to learn. At least the time you spend lost in your phone screen hasn't been wasted."

"Back to my point."

"Of course." Marquis rolled his hands for me to continue. "Do proceed."

"Anyway," I took a breath. "It used to be that *terrific* did mean the same as *terrible*. As in, *I had a terrific headache*." I glanced at an unimpressed Marquis. I started talking faster, so I could get to the cool stuff. "But around the end of the 1800s, *terrific* started to mean *excellent*."

"You don't say." Marquis yawned.

It all made sense to me, because part of me was proud

and happy to be the lead. *Terrific!* And part of me was just plain *terrified*.

Abhi walked by the table.

"Would you like to sit here with us, Abhi?" I asked, syrup dribbling out of the side of my mouth.

"Sure." Abhi's face lightened and she sat. "José is coming back tomorrow."

I was glad, but I had this weird feeling that Mrs. Darling would give the Scrooge role back to El.

"But he still can't be in the play." Marquis sipped his milk.

"Yeah." Abhi nodded, dipped, and chewed. "But I am going to visit him after rehearsal today."

"Why?" I attempted to remove the syrup from my hands with a thin sandpaper napkin.

"He's my friend, and I want him to know he's still my friend, even if he's not Scrooge. Besides, something just doesn't feel right about him being suspended. He really loved being in the play." Abhi dipped her pancake and let it drip. "I can't believe he'd do anything to mess that up."

"Sometimes people make bad choices," Marquis said.

"Well," Abhi said, "I'm going to ask him some questions because I don't believe he clogged that toilet." It sounded like Nancy Drew had a new mystery: *The Secret of the Old Clog.*

"Chewy saw him do it," Marquis said.

Janie walked up. "What are y'all talking about?"

"Abhi wants to go see José after rehearsal today." I wadded up my napkin, not sure how I felt about Abhi visiting El Pollo Loco alone.

"Sure!" Janie nodded. "I'd be glad to come along. He lives on my street."

"That'd be great, Janie." Abhi looked over to me. "Would you like to come?

Before I could answer, Marquis said, "Yes!" I nodded yes, too.

So it was official. After the rehearsal today, Abhi, Janie, Marquis, and I were going to go visit El Pollo Loco's coop.

ωМмт

Later, after English, instead of walking to lunch with Marquis like I usually did, I walked with Abhi, so we could complete Operation Memorize. But since I'm working on it with Abhi, maybe it should be called Operation *Mesmerize*.

Sigh.

Marquis stepped slowly past the table, not making eye contact. I thought he'd sit with us, so I didn't ask him to, and you know what? He walked right past and sat at the table with Sophia, Cliché, and the blue-eye-shadow gang. I was too busy trying to remember the lines I was supposed to say to the Ghost of Christmas Present to think much about it. As I said the line correctly, the next thing I heard was not Abhi reading the line that followed mine, but another voice from behind.

"What?" Janie said her line, sounding like she was hooked up to a sound system. *"Would you so soon snuff out, with your hands, the light I give?"* she bellowed as the Ghost of Christmas Past. She was getting so into her role that she

might actually become a ghost. If it were possible, Janie was almost there.

Everyone turned to see. The clatter of trays and voices were soaked up as if a huge white sponge were standing in the middle of the cafetorium. Janie wore her full costume to lunch: A combination of sheets wrapped her up like an overly toilet-papered house. Layer after layer, the sheer weight of her costume caused her to move sluggishly. Ghostly almost.

But Mrs. Gage wasn't having any of it. Certainly not the bowling ball or the chain, at least one of which could easily be strictly prohibited by the student code of conduct. I'm guessing there's no rule about bowling balls specifically, except what may fall under "general nuisance." That basically meant anything that causes teachers or lunch monitors an annoying pain in the biscuit.

Yes. My mom, who puts the *real* into real estate agent, said, "A contract is a contract." At the beginning of the year, she made me read the whole *Davy Crockett Middle School Code of Student Conduct* before I signed it. Seriously. Then she made me answer questions. "Is it okay to chew gum or bring any candy to school?"

If I answered like a smart aleck, which believe me, I did a few times, she'd make me take three more questions.

Anyway, when it comes to the code of student conduct, I broke the code part. The code wasn't really anything all that mysterious. At school, you're not supposed to do anything besides read, write, and listen. Everything else? A violation of the code of student conduct. Even "grooming that becomes a distraction."

128

Mom had trouble explaining that one. Anyway, I was certain dragging a bowling ball behind you on a loud chain and coming close to people's feet, causing the whole cafeteria to scream, is the definition of *distraction*: "a thing that prevents someone from giving full attention to something else."

Mrs. Gage sent Janie to go unwrap her mummy sheets in the nurse's office.

"She'll be gone for a while," Abhi said, and I nodded.

"I wonder if they'll call her Mummy," I joked. I searched around for Marquis to share a laugh, but he'd already gone.

wwww

Why was it so easy to remember the code of student conduct but not so easy to remember my lines? The play was this Friday, and I was having trouble memorizing my new Scrooge lines.

And today when I got to the bus circle after rehearsal, Marquis wasn't smiling.

"What's the matter?"

"Nothing."

Even though I could tell something was up, I decided to take him at his word, and I told him all about lunch and the line running with Abhi.

He didn't say anything.

"Are you sure everything's okay?" I asked.

"Everything is just fine." Marquis crossed his arms. I believed him until he went off on me a few seconds later. "I have no problem that you dropped me like a bowling ball on the hard cafeteria floor the minute you got a starring role. And when a girl named Abhi came along." He stared at me for a second, and then Marquis turned away. "You've changed."

"It's just for the play."

"I'm *in* the play!" Marquis said to the bus window.

"I know," I said to the back of Marquis's head.

"Do you?"

I wanted to tell him that when I got a new phone, I chose him to call first. I wanted to, but instead my mouth said, "You know what? Forget it!" I don't know if it was the frustration with not being able to memorize my lines or what, but this whole thing was making me mad. Like Scrooge mad.

"Bah! humbug," I mumbled.

Janie and Abhi walked up.

"You two ready to go visit José?" Abhi asked.

"Yes," I said.

"I'm only going because you need a voice of reason," Marquis announced.

Janie slowly put her costume back on as the buses pulled into the circle. "I thought this might cheer El up." Janie smoothed her costume.

This bus driver, Ms. Frances, was nothing like Ms. Nancy. She didn't even notice Abhi wasn't on the right bus. I was pretty sure Ms. Frances was blind. She was always hitting curbs or parking the bus way far away from the curb, so you had to leap down. Anyway, I doubted she'd notice the ghost passenger.

El's coop—or house—sat at the end of Dollarhide Road, a big white rectangle with a flat roof. A blue shutter on one of the windows leaned to the side. We hesitated at the curb, waiting to step into his yard. Abhi wanted to get to the bottom of things. I wasn't sure what Nancy Drew thought we could do. I wasn't sure why I was there either. But we had a ghost with us. What could go wrong?

"It's getting hot under these sheets," Janie announced.

Abhi stepped up on the curb, marched down the sidewalk to the front door, and knocked. We all followed and stood behind her, like a group of kids trying to sell magazines for a youth center. Or a ghost center.

When El opened the door, he leaned on a pair crutches. "Hey, guys! What are *you* doing here?"

"What happened to your leg?" Abhi asked, concern in her voice.

"Oh! That's a long story. I tell you later." El motioned with his hands. "Come in and tell me why y'all are here." On crutches, he led us to an orange-and-white striped couch.

Janie, Abhi, and I sat down.

"I'm so glad to see you guys. I'm so sick of being cooped up in here."

Janie cackled, "The crazy chicken is cooped up." Janie slapped her knee. "That's punny!"

El didn't laugh. He didn't say *justkidding*. He shrugged, then rested his armpits on his crutches. "Take a seat, Marquis."

"I'll stand, if you don't mind." I wondered if Marquis wouldn't even sit because he didn't trust José to tell the truth. He acted like he wouldn't be staying long.

Abhi smiled, looking side to side at us on the couch. "We came by to cheer you up, El."

"Yes," Janie added. "I came in my ghost costume just for you."

We nodded, but everyone knew Janie would look for any excuse to wear a costume.

"How've you been?" Abhi asked.

José sighed. "Bored." He was like a flat soda, no bubbles left.

Silence.

"I miss you guys," José said. "And the play."

We nodded.

"Why'd you do it, José?" Marquis cut to the chase.

"Do what?" José rocked on his crutches. "I *didn't* do any of that stuff they said I did."

"I knew it!" Abhi sat up.

José turned to Abhi. "You did?"

"But Chewy *saw* you do it, José." Marquis shook his head.

"He's lying." El dropped the crutches to the ground, walked to my end of the couch, and said, "Scoot over."

We sucked in our breath as he squeezed between the couch arm and me.

"Hey," Janie said. "I thought you needed those crutches."

"I was just playing around," José said, leaning back on the couch. "Those crutches were from the time I jumped off the roof in fifth grade," he explained. "You know, they won't take crutches back once they're used."

"Did *Chewy* lie?" Marquis crossed his arms. "Or were you just *playing around* when you clogged the toilet with toilet paper?"

"Take it easy, Marquis." Abhi stood, like she was José's defense council. "Let José tell us what happened."

"Yeah!" I nodded. "Judge Joe always gives you a chance to tell your side."

Marquis cut his eyes at me.

"El?" Janie looked down the couch at José. "Maybe it'd help if you told us what you were doing in the restroom all those times you were late to rehearsal."

Silence.

"José?" Abhi's voice floated up. "We're trying to help you."

Were we? I thought to myself. *I thought we were trying to cheer him up, not reenact an episode of* Judge Joe.

"It's embarrassing." José looked at the gold carpet.

In that moment, I thought I might understand. Maybe José didn't like going to the restroom between classes either. Or maybe he clogged the toilet accidentally. I thought I had figured out the mystery of the clogged toilet. "José, I think I know what you're going to say."

"Oh, no!" José grabbed his head. "Did you hear me in there?"

The others' faces scrunched in confusion.

"No," I answered, realizing he thought I had listened to him going to the restroom. "I mean—"

"Okay, okay, I'll tell you," José said, "but promise you won't laugh though."

"I knew it!" Marquis pointed his finger at José.

"Let José finish," Abhi insisted.

"Fine," José said. "I don't like people knowing this because it's kind of dumb. But I'm really superstitious about how and why things happen."

"Well, I'm suspicious. What's your point?" Marquis said.

"Marquis!" we chided.

"Anyway, my superstition made me think I'd have bad luck with the play if I didn't do certain things every day in the same way." José sighed. "I didn't want anyone else to see what I was doing, so I'd go in the boys' room."

"Did you do vocal exercises?" Janie asked, "like saying *red leather, yellow leather* five times fast: *Red leather, yellow leather. Red leather, yellow*—"

134

"Janie!" Marquis interrupted. "Let him talk!"

"Not exactly vocal exercises." José stalled.

Marquis lost his patience. "What do you do *exactly* then?"

"Your honor, Marquis is badgering the witness." We looked around the room. No one was sure who Abhi was talking to.

"Well," José explained, "I got inspired in the audition when I slammed the stage door and yelled, 'I *said* good day!'"

"Oh!" Janie smiled. "I remember that. You were so passionate, El."

"Anyway, Mrs. Darling told me the door slam and the 'Good day!' had gotten me the lead role." José stood and paced. "So once rehearsals started, I got all freaked out and superstitious that if I didn't slam a door and yell, 'I said, *Good day!*' I would have bad luck. I was afraid I'd lose the part. I'm not that good at many things, but I like acting."

"So what's that have to do with clogging toilets in the boy's restroom?" Janie squinted, trying to follow.

"I didn't *do* that!" José's voice rose. "I swear! All I did was slam the stall doors in the bathroom every day before rehearsal. I didn't clog the toilets with toilet paper!"

Abhi nodded like El was making perfect sense.

"Did you yell, 'Good day'?" Janie asked.

"You bet I did," José admitted. "I yelled every time I slammed the stall door. If one time was good, then ten times would be great."

"Except you weren't late the last two days you were in school . . ." Abhi tried to connect the dots. "Instead of hyping yourself up for play practice *after* school, you'd ask to go to the restroom *during* class, so you wouldn't be *late* to rehearsal anymore."

Marquis quizzed Abhi. "Where you coming up with these facts? Did you see any of it? Do you have any evidence at all?"

Abhi turned from Marquis. "Well, it could have happened like that."

"As a matter of fact," José interrupted, "it *did* happen that way. And there *is* a witness."

Everyone gasped and turned toward El, waiting for the surprise witness to be revealed.

"Who?" Marquis demanded.

"Me!" El declared. "Like Abhi said, I had to stop being late because Chewy was all up in my grill. So I did my door slamming and yelling ritual earlier in the day in the privacy of the boys' bathroom!" He looked each of us in the eye. "I was trying to be good. I was trying to be on time. I loved being Scrooge." José choked up. "But when they took me to the office, I was too embarrassed and shocked to explain about my door slamming or to say anything. Besides, Mr. Akins wouldn't have believed me if I had told him, anyway."

"But you're innocent until *proven* guilty!" Abhi shot a look at Marquis. "I rest my case."

"I object!" Marquis yelled. "There's a witness that *saw* the defendant, José, clog the toilets with toilet paper, not slam stall doors."

"That *is* true." Janie nodded, laughing uncomfortably,

sounding unconvinced. "It's the classic case of the assistant director's word against the class clown's."

"Nobody will ever believe me." José sank back in the couch.

"I'm not sure I do," Marquis said. "Sorry."

"Why'd you come then?" José asked.

Marquis shrugged.

"I believe you, El." Abhi sat on the arm of the couch next to José and patted his shoulder.

El swallowed. "Thank you."

Abhi and El turned toward Janie and me.

"It's getting hot in here," Janie said. She stood and fled, walking toward the door and opening it. She hummed as she began unraveling her sheets.

Now I was the only one left on the jury.

"What do you say, Zack?" Marquis, my best friend, asked.

"Yeah, Zack, what do you say?" Abhi, my I-don't-know-what, asked.

"Do you believe me?" José pleaded with his puppy dog eyes.

But Chewy saw him.

El, Abhi, and Marquis looked at me.

Waiting.

"Well." José sounded defeated. "It's not worth all the trouble. Let's just drop it and move on."

"No, El," Abhi's voice rose. "We—"

"Please!" El said. "Let's just forget about it."

"I believe you," I interrupted, and I did, mostly.

CHAPTER 26
EXTRA DRAMA

Wednesday was El's first day back at school after his suspension. At lunch, Abhi and El sat with Marquis and me. Abhi and José were happy. Happy El was back at school. Happy that I believed El.

But Marquis was *not* so happy about that. And he was *really* not happy that Mrs. Darling argued to Mr. Akins that José should be allowed to return to the play and participate backstage. Mr. Akins finally agreed as long as José's punishment of not acting in the play was kept. Mrs. Darling invited El to be an assistant to the stage manager.

"That's not right," Marquis said. "I don't trust him like I trust Chewy. Why would Chewy lie?"

I sat there. I didn't know the answer to that one.

From behind me, Janie put her hands on my shoulders. "You're king of the world," she said, which she followed with, "*Titanic*, nineteen ninety-seven, starring . . . *sigh* . . . Leo DiCaprio. He's dreamy."

She was right.

Not that Leonardo DiCaprio was dreamy, but that I couldn't even think of more that I could wish for. Abhi hung out with me now. I was the lead in the play. José could now be at school again. But when he asked me how rehearsal was going I noticed how sad his brown eyes could get. I think maybe happy people can get the saddest.

And another thing also bugged me. I was so tired from all the rehearsals, line memorizing, special visits, and entertaining lunches, that I could barely keep my eyes open.

I drifted off, then jerked awake.

I was struggling to get through the day without falling asleep and tried to remember there were only two more rehearsals until Friday. Tomorrow would be the dress rehearsal. If I could make it three more days, then I could rest.

wWMm

Later that day, at the end of a pretty good rehearsal, Mrs. Darling said, "Take a seat for an announcement."

"I hope she's going to announce that they're reopening the investigation of the framing of José Soto," Abhi grumbled.

I didn't say much. I wanted to explain to her that we're not on a cold-case file show or in one of her Nancy Drew novels. But I didn't.

We didn't have time for all *that* drama in the drama

club. Besides, when we had visited him at his house, El had told us to leave it alone. But Abhi was having trouble doing that. Abhi still thought something fishy had happened. I practically had to sit on her lap to keep her from taking on Blythe when she attempted to refuse El as her new assistant to the stage manager.

Marquis thought José wanted us to leave it alone because he was guilty, and we'd all find out he was lying if we kept digging.

"Since our performance of *A Christmas Carol* occurs during the school day on Friday, several of your parents asked if we could have an additional performance Thursday evening at five, so they could come without missing work," Mrs. Darling said.

All I heard was "additional performance." The blood drained from my head.

"We are inviting your parents to come to the final dress rehearsal at 5:00 p.m. tomorrow." Mrs. Darling handed Chewy the invitations to distribute.

At first Abhi wouldn't take hers as Chewy stood there holding it out in front of her. "Did Blythe get you to do it?"

"Do what?" Chewy paused, confused.

"Let it go, Abhi," El said, resting his hand on hers.

Chewy continued handing the invitations out. Abhi watched Blythe like a hawk, but Blythe just scribbled something in her notebook.

Mrs. Darling interrupted the outburst of excitement about our parents being able to come to dress rehearsal. "First, we have a show to make work, so study those lines."

She looked right at me.

Seriously.

"Be on time tomorrow. This is no dress rehearsal!" Blythe yelled from the wings.

"But it *is*," Abhi mumbled. "It *actually* is."

"Hey!" I got an idea to cheer Abhi up. "Do you have a cell phone? Because I could call you to practice if you did." I was getting good at coming up with excuses to get closer to Abhi.

"Sure," Abhi said.

She took my hand in hers.

I gulped.

Seriously.

Then she wrote her name and number in pen on my open palm.

That happened.

She touched my skin by hand and by pen.

I stood there.

This was more than I had hoped for.

Wondering how long I could keep her handwriting on my palm, I stared at her number and name. Now that's *hand*writing!

"Earth to Zack?" Abhi's voice broke the spell. "What are we going to do about Blythe?" Abhi was convinced Blythe had something to do with José's unfortunate suspension from school and from the play.

"Remember, José asked us to drop it." I tilted my head to the side. I wasn't so sure Nancy Drew was going to. But I also wasn't sure why Chewy would lie anyway. Why would he?

I really wanted to make Abhi feel better, but if it turned out José was innocent, would Mrs. Darling give back his role? If I were honest, I *was* worried about losing my role, losing all the good stuff that was happening. I want this to last. Selfish. Self-centered. I was heartless Scrooge, out for myself.

Oh man, and José even said he learned all the lines and his blocking while he was suspended. I did notice him, sad-eyed, moving his mouth when I said my lines.

But what could I do?

That night in bed, nervous sweat soaked my sheets.

I wanted to text Marquis, but he doesn't have a phone. You'd think once you get a phone all your problems would be solved. But then people like Marquis and Janie don't have phones. Abhi gave me her number today, so I texted her. No big deal. I just needed someone to text. Besides, I was worried about her and the whole José situation, which is practically all she talked about.

OMG! She's writing me back. I smiled, remembering the time we sat together on the bus. Suddenly the speech bubble with the ellipsis that means she's responding disappeared.

I tried to refresh my phone, but still no answer.

I checked the clock on my phone: 8:37.

I kept my message app open to my conversation with Abhi, which really wasn't a conversation because there weren't two voices. I refreshed again: 8:38.

I didn't feel like talking, just texting. It was easier to text because you had time to think about what you say. I wished I could text Marquis, so he'd calm me down. Plus, he's a little mad at me for believing José. Unlike Abhi, I wasn't 100 percent sure he was innocent. But, unlike Marquis, I wasn't 100 percent sure he was guilty. I was like 51 percent sure something wasn't right about the whole José-clogged-the-toilet suspension issue, and 49 percent sure José just went too far with a prank.

I refreshed my phone. I saw the speech bubble again, as if Abhi were replying and starting my first text-versation "with" Abhi. But again, as fast as the speech bubble appeared, it vanished.

I texted again.

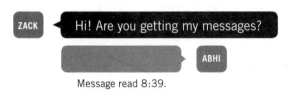

ZACK Hi! Are you getting my messages?

ABHI

Message read 8:39.

Bubbles.

Blank.

Sigh.

Maybe my phone wasn't connected to the Internet. I checked. It was.

I needed someone—anyone—to respond to me. With no one else to text, I texted Mom. What? I needed a distraction. I could've been studying my lines, but instead I texted Mom.

ZACK Night, Mom.

MOM I'm just in the other room, Sweetie. Do you really need to text me?

ZACK Um . . . yeah.

MOM Okay, g'night. Can I at least come by and give u a hug?

ZACK I guess ;-)

Mom and I hugged it out, but I felt too stupid to ask her why Abhi wasn't texting me back. The whole time Mom was in my room, I wanted to keep checking my phone. But I restrained myself. I only checked my messages three times.

"What are you checking your phone for? Messages?"

"Nothing." I dropped the phone on the bed.

"Zack?"

"Nothing!" I didn't want Mom to know that her son was such a dork that people didn't even reply to his texts. And that I really should be learning my lines, but all I could think about was when Abhi was going to text me back.

"I can see something's bothering you," Mom said. "I know I'm your mom, but I know stuff."

I felt guilty. The only reason I was following José's direction to drop investigating his case is I wanted to be

Scrooge. If he *was* innocent, I'd probably lose my role and be Tiny Tim again. Was I turning into a selfish Scrooge again, only caring about myself?

Fifty-one percent of myself said *yes*.

"I'm just not feeling confident, Mom. That's all."

"Is that all?" Mom smiled. "I learned this thing on the Internet. Two minutes to confidence. And it works. Want to try it?"

I shrugged. What did I have to lose? I stood.

"Okay, so you just change the way you stand for two minutes." Mom raised her arms into a victory *V.* "Like this. Now you do it."

I felt stupid, but I was desperate, so I raised my arms up into a *V.*

"Now, tilt your chin back and let's hold this pose for two minutes."

I did.

"For some reason, when your body is in a strong position, it releases different chemicals, and you change from the outside in," Mom explained, still in a *V.* "Fake it till you make it!"

As I listened to Mom explain how we are influenced by how we hold our body, I held the *V* and hoped it would work.

"Okay, two minutes are up. How do you feel?"

I wanted to say I didn't feel anything.

But I did.

"I'm going to go read over my lines."

"Good plan, Zack." Mom squeezed me extra tightly. "I do love you."

"I know." I hugged her tight for longer than usual. "I love you too, Mom."

When the door shut, I opened my script. As I studied my lines, I realized all the work Abhi and I had done had paid off. I already knew my lines. I just needed the confidence to *know* I knew them. I'd be fine at Thursday's dress rehearsal/performance for parents, and I'd be fine for Friday's performance for the student body of Davy Crockett Middle School, in the last period of the day. I couldn't keep worrying about Abhi worrying about El. He did ask us to leave it alone, and he must have had his reasons. Besides, all I was really worried about at that point was whether Abhi would text me back.

I still checked my phone about a hundred times.

No message.

I fell asleep in the *V* pose.

Ding . . . ding . . . ding!

I would've practiced my lines last night if I had known Abhi wasn't planning on texting me back till the next day. At least I hoped it was Abhi!

I felt around in my sheets and pillow for the phone. I found it under my pillow. 6:03 a.m.! I was stiff from falling asleep in the *V* pose, and so sleepy I could barely focus.

"Rise and shine, child of mine!" Mom pounded on my door. "Zack?" Mom tapped again, lightly. "Wakey! Wakey!"

I sprang from under the comforter to read my messages from Abhi. As I'd hoped, three messages. All from Abhi. All in a row.

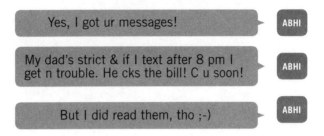

The door creaked open, and Mom saw me sitting on the edge of my bed, smiling back at the smile emoji Abhi had sent. "It's a miracle! He has risen!"

I yawned and stretched my arms, with my phone in one hand.

"Oh, I see," Mom said, "so checking for phone messages is worth waking up for. I guess your ol' Mom and Dad should've gotten you a phone years ago."

"Yep." I instinctively pulled my phone down, so Mom couldn't see the screen.

"So is that how it's going to be?" Mom laughed. "Who is she, Zack?"

"Nobody." I shrugged. "I've got to get in the shower."

"Yes, you do," Mom agreed.

I dragged past her, rubbing my eyes.

"Hey, sleepyhead," Mom teased. "Don't take your phone in the shower."

"Very funny, Mom." I said. But I was so tired I might have. I kept nodding off while I stood in the shower. I rested my head on the cold tile as the hot water beat down on me, lulling me into shutting my eyes.

∿∿∿

Dad had offered to drive me to school on his way to his job at the Instant Lube because Mom had to meet a client early Thursday morning. It was dress rehearsal/parent performance day. Both Mom and Dad were coming to support me at 5, so I wanted to do a good job.

Dad swigged his enormous Bill Miller travel mug of coffee, which was the size of the trashcan in our bachelor bathroom. Seriously.

"Does that coffee make you awake?" I asked.

Dad laughed. "I couldn't make it through the morning without it."

"Can I try some?" I asked, trying to sound only a little interested, so he'd let me.

"Sure." Dad lifted the trashcan of coffee over to me.

Once he had his eyes on the road I guzzled as much as I could. After awhile, Dad looked over. "Take it easy, Z!"

Oh God, was it ever hot, but I couldn't act like it'd scorched my throat. Sweat beaded on my forehead. I wiped it away with the sleeve of the flannel shirt I was wearing.

"How 'bout another swig, Daddy-O?"

"All right." Dad handed the coffee over. "But be careful. Bill Miller makes it strong. This will be your last sip."

"Okay." I guzzled down the rest of the coffee as Dad had to deal with a tricky intersection. A minute later, I handed the empty container back to Dad.

"Hey!" Dad shook the mug. "This is empty!"

"Sorry, Dad!" I said. "I guess I got carried away."

"Phttt!" Dad made that sound when he was mad.

I loosened my collar and rolled up my sleeves. Besides feeling hot, I didn't really notice how different I felt until I leapt from the van like a spring.

"Zack?" Dad yelled after me. "You forgot to close the door!"

As I spun around, it was as if I became lighter, and in two steps I returned and slammed the door with a bang. I guess besides energy, coffee gives you superhuman strength. I liked this feeling. I was on. O-N. On. On. On. On. ON! I practically danced to class. Bill Miller *did* make strong coffee.

I smiled at Marquis and he smiled back, and for some reason, everything Janie did, instead of getting on my nerves, was hilarious. In math, Janie ghosted herself and tried to convince Mr. Gonzalez, "I'm dressed as a ghost so kids will know not to be scared of math. Ghost math, minus the BOO!" she shouted.

I burst out laughing. Only Marquis joined me.

Ignoring me, Mr. Gonzalez answered Janie algebraically, "*X* doesn't equal *Y*."

"Why not?"

"Not *Why*." He wrote $x \neq y$ on the board. "The letter *Y*!"

"Math ruins everything." Janie tried to sit, but her costume was too thick from being wrapped around her too many times. "Maybe I got carried away with the sheets today."

"Humbug," Marquis said.

I leaned toward Janie. "He's saying what you said isn't true."

"Yeah, it doesn't add up," Marquis said.

"Extra credit for Marquis on math humor." Mr. G. smiled.

"Wait?" My face squinted. "What?" I didn't get the joke, but I was starting to get a headache. And I felt irritated, all of a sudden.

"What about *my* math humor?" Janie whined.

"Just me and my Alge-bros," Marquis said.

José didn't say a word. He just sat there and didn't participate in the math humor. The new El was humorless.

"Oh, brother!" Abhi said.

"Oh, sis-TAH!" Marquis said.

"Marquis is on fire today," Mr. Gonzalez said.

I racked my brain to find something funny to say, but my brain's coffee battery was on low.

José put his head down, which looked like a pretty tempting thing to do.

wwwm

I was worse by the end of math. My head throbbed. My energy left. And everything Janie did worked my nerves again. Janie whipped her sheet in the air, ready to ghost herself.

Chewy yanked the sheet out of her hands. "No way, Missy!" Talk about a Ghostbuster.

Blythe stood behind, observing, nodding approval, straightening her sweater, smiling. She caught me looking at her. "Zack, you don't look so good."

I tried to muster a comeback, but nothing came, except a burp.

151

~~~~~

After school, I dragged myself to dress rehearsal when I really just wanted to be in bed. But it was the final rehearsal before the parent performance tonight. I felt like I was only half awake, and I had to do two full performances.

Before our first rehearsal, I hid in the wings and tried to get myself pumped up. I was even willing to try those confidence stances mom taught me. I spread my arms up in a *V*, high to the sky, hoping my confidence and energy would rise. About a minute into my power pose, Chewy walked up, but Blythe lingered behind him like a fart. I held my stance. I needed all that I could get. Sure, it was embarrassing, but this is my last chance to be off script, to fix everything, to become Scrooge, and not make a fool of myself in front of a huge audience tonight. And I'd just have to think about tomorrow *tomorrow*.

Blythe shoved Chewy toward me.

"I don't know if that warm-up stance is sanctioned," Chewy said. His voice squeaked on the last word.

Blythe was a puppeteer, pulling Chewy's strings, like some mob boss lying low, controlling things from the jail of the dark wings of the cafetorium stage.

"Sanctioned?" My jaw dropped, but I kept my arms up high and my chin tilted back. If anybody had walked up, it would've appeared as if I was being arrested. "I don't even know what that means."

"What?" Chewy asked, turning toward Blythe, fidgeting.

"C'mon, Chewy. You said it. What does the word *sanctioned* mean?" I pressed him because I had figured out what was going down.

Just as I'd predicted, Chewy shuffled over to Blythe, who tried motioning him away with her sweater stumps, but Chewy skittered straight to her. Maybe Abhi was right. Maybe Blythe was some behind-the-scenes puppeteer getting Chewy to do whatever she wanted. Could she be behind the frame-up? Was there even a frame-up?

"But I need some information to complete the order you gave me!" Chewy explained. Blythe walked around the whole back of the stage, trying to escape Chewy, but she couldn't.

Obviously, Blythe had enlisted Chewy to be the cop she couldn't be.

I held my stance, arms spread in a *V* for victory for the entire two minutes, ready to get my Scrooge on. As the final dress rehearsal dragged on, my ragged nerves from the coffee crash made me more and more crotchety, and the crash was unexpectedly working like a charm, if the charm had nasty coffee breath.

"By Jove, whatever you've done, Zack, keep doing it," Mrs. Darling cheered between scenes.

What had I *done*?

No sleep. Check.

A trash can of coffee. Check.

Oh, and I almost forgot—my victory pose.

I was now a worn-out, crotchety old man. I *was* Scrooge.

153

When we finished, Mrs. Darling walked down the center of the cafetorium toward the stage. "Brava! And Bravo!"

"What does that mean?" I asked.

"In the thea–TUH, when a performance by a woman is as fantastic as I have just now witnessed, then we say 'Brava.'" She motioned toward Abhi, Cliché, and Janie. Then she motioned toward Marquis and me. "And for the young men, I say 'Bravo.'"

"That's like the male and female word endings in Spanish too, Mrs. Darling," Janie said.

Now I knew exactly how to prepare for the big day tomorrow. I just had to figure out how I'd get the coffee I needed. Mom would never let me have coffee, so I had to real-world problem-solve like in math.

The parent performance of the show went well, too. I got all my lines. I didn't ask for a line one time. Mom, Dad, and some of the other parents who came gave us a standing ovation. Mrs. Darling had trained us to do our bows. It felt great getting clapped for, but inside my brain was on full grouch.

"Hey, Zack DelaSCROOGE," José walked up with his hand out. "Good show! He shook my hand and looked me in the eyes. "I can't think of anyone who I'd want to take over my role than you. You were awesome. I mean it."

And he did. I *believed* him.

"So nice to see you two getting along." Janie walked up and smiled. "It's a Christmas miracle. 'He puzzled and puzzled till his puzzler was sore. Then the Grinch thought of something he hadn't before. Maybe Christmas, he thought . . . doesn't come from a store. Maybe Christmas, perhaps . . . means a little bit more!' from *How the Grinch Stole Christmas,* nineteen sixty-six, narrated by Boris Karloff."

Again, José had no comment. He just yawned.

Mom walked up in her Century 21 gold jacket, holding a tray of orange sections. "Good show, Actin' Alamos."

Dad stood a few feet behind her. "Yeah, guys. Good show!" He stepped forward and gave me the hard and stiff man handshake. "You made me so proud."

"We've got quite the actor," Mom said, placing the tray of oranges on a table. "Here are some refreshments for all of your hard work. Y'all were all great. I can't believe this is middle school and not Broadway."

Like a bunch of vultures, the cast and crew surrounded the tray of oranges and devoured everything there. José even sucked on the paper towel that had lined the plate.

"I'm getting all the orange juice that's left," José said, talking with a paper towel in his mouth. At least sugar brought him back to the surface, if only for a little while.

"Glad you liked them," Mom said. Our eyes met, and I knew she knew this had to be El Pollo Loco. José offered to return the paper towel when he was finished, but Mom just turned away like she didn't notice.

"Thank you, Ms. Murray," Abhi said. She didn't say *Mrs. Delacruz.* I had only told her my Mom's last name once. I wouldn't have expected her to remember—unless maybe I was important to her.

Marquis side-hugged my mom. "Thanks for the oranges."

"I like Marquis getting his vitamin C." Ma, Marquis's grandma, said as she approached slowly.

The other kids thanked Mom, too—after Mrs. Darling told them to.

Dad stood back, like he was shy, like he didn't know what to do. I knew he was proud, and I was glad the performance had gone so well. I needed to remember that sometimes trying new things turns out good, even when you're not sure they will.

CHAPTER 28
THE RAW DEAL

"**E**xcuse me, sir?" Mom gently shook me awake. I could smell her hand lotion. "Are you the famous *Zack*-tor I've been hearing so much about?"

"Oh, Mom, *puh*-lease!" I said. "That was *so* weak."

When I slowly stood, I was stiff and could barely keep my eyes open. Come to think of it, two nights without much sleep made me feel like I was slogging through mud. But I had a plan.

I waited till Mom was in the shower. I tiptoed into the kitchen and filled a glass halfway with almond milk, and then I dug three heaping scoops out of Mom's coffee. I didn't have time to figure out how to make coffee, so I'd go straight to the source. I never heard of raw coffee, but sometimes fighters on the Mixed Martial Arts drink raw eggs for strength. I stirred the coffee grounds and almond milk up really fast, but it still had little black dots floating in it, looking like cookies-and-cream ice cream. I stirred it as much as I could and swigged it down as if I were dying of thirst.

Ugh.

It tasted like almond milk with Grandpa's ashtray dumped in. I wanted to spit it out, but I poured in more milk and stirred again. I heard Mom getting out of the shower. A clump of coffee grounds clung to the bottom of my glass like mud, refusing to mix. Quickly, I spooned up the clump and ate the gritty coffee sludge. I even had to chew some. I forced myself to swallow.

Double *ugh!*

I rinsed out the glass (and my mouth) to clear away any evidence. I spit in the stainless-steel sink and rinsed it all down the drain. I'd seen forensics on TV. I was no amateur.

"What's going on in here?" Mom said, looking at her coffee container on the counter. "Look at that, Zack. You got my coffee out for me."

"Wha?" I stuttered, tracing my teeth with my tongue to get rid of any stray grounds. "Oh, yeah, of course. Um." I smiled. "You know, random acts of kindness."

"And you rinsed the glass and put in on the rack to dry." Mom pretended to have a heart attack, grabbing at her gold jacket, falling against the cabinets. "What have you done with my son, Zack? Who are you?"

"Mom, you're overacting, and that's unattractive." I bent down and tied my shoes. "Even Mrs. Darling would tell you to hold back a tetch."

As I finished getting dressed, the coffee started pulsing through my system. And this time, since the coffee wasn't hot, neither was I. *I'm a genius*, I thought to myself. I checked myself in the mirror and then danced my way to the door.

"What's gotten into you, Zack?" Mom opened the front door.

I burst through the door and popped my victory pose. "I'm a supah stah!"

Mom squinted at me as I bounced like a tennis ball down the driveway to the Honda.

At school, the first half of the day sped past—breakfast through lunch bounced by coffee-quick. It was *Friday.* It was the *day* before the winter holi*day.* And, most important, it was performance *day*—last period. That meant no gym, which meant no laps or sit-ups, so pretty much it was a perfect day.

The only bad part was El and Abhi were still sad about the whole suspension-from-the-play thing.

"I just wish there was something we could do," Abhi said.

"But please don't," José urged her. "I just want this whole thing behind me."

That's right. He said *behind* and didn't make a butt joke. He really was down.

I had to stop Abhi from going to Mr. Akins several

times, then to Mrs. Darling. She even wanted to see if Mrs. Harrington would help.

I nodded. "But he asked us not to."

Marquis agreed. "We don't really know what happened."

"I know . . . " Abhi's voice trailed off, sad and defeated.

All I could do was be a friend. We asked José to sit with us at lunch. He did, but he hardly ate his macaroni and cheese. Who doesn't eat macaroni and cheese?

Other than that, the coffee concoction kept me moving at a rapid pace. Marquis and I kept giggling at how peppy and loud I was. Once I even saw El and Abhi crack a smile when I couldn't stop bouncing my leg in English.

When I told Marquis and Janie about my special recipe, they couldn't believe it.

"You did what?" Marquis shook his head. "You are straight-up loony tunes!"

Of course Janie had a quote from a show. "'Double, double toil and trouble; Fire burn, and caldron bubble.' From the witches of *Macbeth* by William Sssshakesspeare."

Even Janie talking with a British accent didn't bother me. And she'd been doing it all day.

"I'd do anything to make me a better Scrooge," I said. And I would've.

I also knew from experience that my Scrooge rebound— the jittery, tired, edgy post-coffee crash—wouldn't hit till after lunch. This would get me to my peak of grouchiness in time for my performance. Toward the end of lunch, my transformation began.

"Do you have to talk so loud ALL the time?" I snapped

at Janie. My head throbbed. "I'm sorry," I said, but I wasn't, or was I? I couldn't stop it. I was becoming Scrooge.

"Fare thee well," Janie said. "I know it is only thy potion talking."

I picked up my tray and stormed off. When Marquis tried to pat me on the back as we went to math, I winced and pulled away.

"Okay, Scrooge," Marquis said with a smirk. "Save some for the stage."

wwwm

My mood shifted even more when Mr. Gonzalez had me stay behind to finish some polynomials.

"When am I ever going to use this?" I growled.

"You need to subtract some of that attitude, Mr. Delacruz!" Mr. Gonzalez gave me *the* look. "I'm trying to keep you from blowing your grade in math for the semester."

"Okay, okay," I conceded. But I wasn't okay. Staying behind meant I didn't leave with the rest of the cast and crew, which made me even grouchier. They left class early to get ready for the play. So I was already behind, and I needed to get there before I got sent to the office for my caffeinated mouth. *Raw coffee must be different,* I thought.

After I handed Mr. Gonzalez his worksheet back, the excitement of heading out to get ready for the play made me slam the door a bit harder than I needed to.

I waited to hear Mr. Gonzalez yell my name, but instead I heard a rumble in my tummy. And it wasn't just an embarrassing noise like at the audition. This sound had pressure and power and feeling. It was like a loud, angry family was moving furniture downstairs in my stomach.

Warmth covered me like a wet sheet. Then the chills. I leaned against the wall. My stomach's growling and moaning echoed through the empty sixth-grade hall. The coffee concoction had hit me in a way I hadn't expected. Sure, I was moody. But now molten mocha lava rolled through me like I was a volcano. Lava bubbled, rumbled, and pushed its way down.

I sprinted for the very *place* to do the very *thing* I'd so far been able to avoid. But there was no choice. Butt Mountain was about to blow its top.

I tightened every muscle I had, walking on my toes, holding off the eruption as long as I could. Each Frankenstein step threatened to release the dangerous, toxic flow of raw coffee and almond milk that moved through me, ready to escape.

I shoved open the door to the boy's restroom, threw open the stall, and landed on the cool seat seconds before the eruption.

If this were a real volcano, it would have destroyed a forest, flattened buildings, and mummified running dogs like Mount Vesuvius did in Pompeii.

And as suddenly as it had started, it ended.

There I sat on the toilet. I sighed in relief. I'd made it. Or had I?

I reached into the plastic toilet paper dispenser, looking for what you'd expect. I panicked as my hand moved deeper and deeper into the empty dispenser. No paper.

Not one square.

I couldn't risk pulling up my pants and getting lava on them and my underwear, so I left them around my ankles, like prison shackles, and shuffled from stall to stall to stall. No toilet paper. Not a square to spare. Just like I'd said to Mom a week ago—there's never any toilet paper in the boys' room.

I felt faint.

At that moment, I was already late to get into my Scrooge makeup and costume. I knew the bell would ring any minute, and everyone would see me with my pants down. Literally. I'd be the new Poops McGillicutty.

But suddenly I remembered something! In the panic, I'd forgotten that Mom had given me those wipes. And I'd forgotten that I had them with me. I didn't know how I could have forgotten. It was like walking around with a box of Kleenex in my pants.

I shuffled back to my stall and pulled the wipes out of my pocket and did clean-up duty. I used the whole pack, and I worried the toilet would clog.

I flushed and watched the bowl fill up, but then the water went down and every last one of those three-ply wipes disappeared.

No clog.

Hmmmm.

That was strange. Chewy claimed he had seen El clog the toilet with handfuls of toilet paper. But even a whole package of the heavy-duty wipes didn't clog the toilet.

That didn't make any sense. Toilet tissue is way thinner, and let's not forget the fact that there never is any.

Thinking about the inconsistency of Chewy's story,

I absent-mindedly washed my hands. I grabbed a paper towel to dry off and . . . then it hit me.

Paper towels!

I grabbed a paper towel.

And another.

And another.

Paper towels kept coming out with each yank till I had a wad the size of a softball. *That should do it*, I thought. *I'll run a little test.* These paper towels were so much heavier than even the three-ply wipes.

I dropped the wad of paper towels into the water, and flushed. Unlike the wipes, instead of going down, the water and paper towels filled the bowl slowly. Once the water reached the rim, it didn't stop. Water floated over the edge and splashed on the floor.

A bell went off in my head, and in the hall. I ran out of the bathroom and toward destiny.

CHAPTER 30
THE GOOD SHOW GIFT

When I walked into the dressing room, which was also the janitor's closet, the smell of old mop, stage makeup, and Abhi greeted me.

"Zack, I got you this." Abhi placed a red carnation in my open hand. "Good show!"

"I got you something," I said, "but I'll give it to you later."

"What are you up to, Zack Delacruz?" Abhi raised her eyebrows.

I leaned down and whispered into her ear. "To get your present, you have to meet me in the wings by the curtain rope during the final scene."

"Okay." Abhi nodded slowly.

I patted her on the back. "And bring those Nancy Drew skills, too."

I turned to the cast. "Has anybody seen El?"

"I think I saw him backstage," Marquis said, adjusting his costume. "Shouldn't you be getting in costume, my friend?"

"I'll take my costume with me." I grabbed the hanger with Scrooge's first costume.

Abhi smoothed her long red dress. "I hope you can cheer him up. I've tried everything."

"I'll try," I said, smiling to myself.

I found El backstage, sitting in a chair, staring into space. "Hey, El. I've been looking for you."

"Do you have something I can do? I'm bored. Blythe told me to help Chewy pull the curtain up and down." José lowered his head. "But he wouldn't let me help."

"Actually, I've got a plan I think you're going to like." I grinned.

He sat up and listened.

"I think you are innocent, but I am going to need your help to prove it," I said.

"Thanks, but I don't want to cause any trouble," José said.

"The trouble is your name has to be cleared. And I'm doing it whether you help or not."

"Okay, Zack." José squeezed his eyes shut. "What do you need me to do?"

"Do you remember your Scrooge lines?" I asked.

"You know I do."

"Good." I nodded. "I need you to play Scrooge."

"Wha'?"

"You earned this role, and I think someone is trying to

sabotage you," I said. "I think I can prove it, but you have to play the role you were meant to play."

"Well." He took the hangers from me, grinning. "If it's what you want! But shouldn't we tell someone?"

I shrugged. "We're out of time."

José disappeared behind the curtain.

I turned and saw Cliché.

"I heard everything."

"That was between José and me." I stepped closer to Cliché.

"I have only one condition for my silence." She held out the Tiny Tim costume and looked me up and down. She pushed it toward me, raising an eyebrow. "I didn't want to dress like a boy anyway."

"It's curtain time!" Chewy ran by. "I'm in charge of the curtain! Clear the way!"

I took the costume from Cliché.

Mrs. Darling clapped her hands together. "Cast and crew, wherever you are." Mrs. Darling stage-whispered, "Have a good show, Actin' Alamos. I am so proud of you. Each and every one of you."

"Even *me*?" José yelled from the dressing room/ janitor's closet.

"Even *you*, Mr. Soto," Mrs. Darling said. "Now, I'll be out in the audience. If I put my hand up to my ear, it means I want you to . . ."

"Project!" We finished her sentences by now. We were ready.

"Very well," Mrs. Darling said, sticking her head out between the curtains and inspecting the crowd. "Looks like all the audience has settled in. Places, everyone! Places!"

I peeked around the curtain and saw Mrs. Harrington *shhh*-ing the audience. I hoped she'd be proud of what I was about to do, because there would be no taking it back once it began.

The time had arrived. Goose bumps covered my arms.

Chewy strained to lift the curtain. His feet lifted off the stage floor a few times. I thought he might fly into the air like Peter Pan. But before I knew it, the curtain was up.

José stood in the center of the stage as Scrooge. The stage lights burned in the silence.

José said Scrooge's first line.

Whew!

Surprised to see José playing Scrooge, Marquis stumbled over his first line, but he recovered quickly.

Sorry buddy, I just had to right a wrong.

After the shock of seeing José playing Scrooge, the play went as planned. Though I wasn't sure what Mrs. Darling would think, I felt pretty sure she'd understand after I explained.

Later, when Janie's sheet-wrapped Ghost of Christmas Past made her entrance, dragging a bowling ball on a chain, everybody laughed. I suppose we should've expected that.

I remembered every line Tiny Tim had and his blocking, like a good alternate, though wearing a costume fitted for Cliché was awkward. Whenever I tried to move, the pants gave me a wedgie. But when I saw José on stage, walking and talking as Scrooge, I knew I had done the right thing.

I felt this proud, nervous, happy feeling. Backstage,

Abhi walked up and hugged me. I guessed she liked my gift: José playing his rightful role.

The show was going on without any problem.

But like Cliché says, "It's not over till it's over." During the play's last scene, something occurred that no amount of literary element knowledge could have foreshadowed. This happening would go down in history. It would be remembered by the Fightin' Alamos for years to come. The stuff of legends.

"Abhi." I lowered my chin. "It's time."

She nodded, and the two of us walked up to Chewy, blocking his view of the stage. We were a wall of truth, and Chewy was about to smack into it.

"Excuse me," Chewy whispered. "The play's almost over. I need to see the stage so I can lower the curtain."

"Not so fast, Bub." Abhi held her palm up. "We want to talk to you first."

"I'm busy!" Chewy gripped the curtain rope.

"It'll only take a second," I began. "Chewy, we're all friends here."

Abhi scowled.

"I believe you witnessed one José Soto '*stuffing* handfuls of toilet tissue into the toilet' on or about the second week of November."

Chewy looked from side to side and then swallowed. "That sounds about right."

"And did you, or did you not, lie about the *method* of clogging?" My co-counsel Abhi continued.

"The *method*?" Chewy asked. "I'm not sure what you're getting at."

"In fact, wasn't it *you*, Chewy"—I stepped closer, my hands clasped behind my back—"who was angry because of a smack to the head by an out-of-control snowflake? Wasn't it you, Chewy, who had an insatiable hunger for power that left *you* with no other option but to stuff the toilet with paper towels?"

"I . . . I . . ." Chewy stammered, fidgeting with the curtain rope. "I don't recall."

"Because, *in fact*, Davy Crockett's sixth-grade toilets have been rigorously tested and, *in fact*, they do *not* clog with toilet paper of any kind." I held up a paper towel.

Chewy gasped.

"In fact, the toilets *only* clog with handfuls of the thicker, more absorbent and scratchy paper towels found by the sink. Isn't that right, Chewy!"

Chewy started to stammer. "I . . . I . . . I . . ." He looked around.

"Where you looking, Chewy? Looking for an exit? Or are you looking for Blythe?" Abhi questioned. "Is *she* behind this? Did she put you up to it? Tell us; we can protect you. Are you her puppet, Chewy?"

"She's in the bathroom. She's behind nothing." Sweat glistened on his forehead.

On stage, the play was at its climax, the highest point, the moment of truth the audience had been waiting for. Will Ebenezer Scrooge finally change who he has been and open his heart to save Tiny Tim's life?

"AND I AM NOT A PUPPET! I WAS DOING *MY* JOB!" Chewy exploded, loud enough that he could be heard by the entire cafetorium. He didn't care. Chewy spit out his confession: "Blythe doesn't control me! I was tired of her always taking my role, taking what was mine! And it was all José's fault. Never on time, never paying attention, always slapping people's faces while pretending to be a snowflake. I took care of it all. But do you appreciate me? Do you respect me? NO!" His voice grew loud and shrill. He didn't even notice that the actors had stopped performing and everyone was listening to him yell. "I'm the assistant director, I'm making this play work, and nobody's taking credit for MY JOB!" Chewy screamed so loud, Abhi and I spun around to see how José and Janie reacted to the disturbance in the wings.

Janie tried to get the show back on track, but she was so thrown off by Chewy's outburst that she stumbled on the chain connected to the bowling ball wrapped around her legs. As she tumbled to the ground, the bowling ball broke off the chain and rolled into the wings.

Wub . . . wub . . . wub . . . wub.

The audience laughed.

To my surprise, the ball struck Chewy and knocked him over like a bowling pin, which in turn caused him to yank the curtain rope, which started something he wouldn't be able to finish. The curtain raced down toward the floor, and Chewy, still clinging to the rope, flew up toward the ceiling.

The curtain contraption unwound quickly, howling as it dropped from up high. Everybody screamed when the mess of fabric smashed on the stage, inches from where Janie and José had stood.

The force from the curtain landing propelled Chewy up even more, swinging him from above the stage to above the audience. Holding on to the rope he looked like a human tetherball.

We all stood on the stage, tracking Chewy's flight as he swung above the audience again at a greater speed and height.

What had my plan to clear El's name done?

I knew I might have killed the show by switching parts, but I hoped I didn't kill Chewy too. Even though he framed El, he didn't deserve to die.

Mrs. Harrington turned on all the lights. Above the cafetorium, Chewy screamed at her, "But that's my jooooooooooooOOOOOOOOOOOB!"

CHAPTER 31

THE ROLE OF A LIFETIME

Screech!

"Come down from there, this very instant, Mr. Johnson!" Mr. Akins spoke firmly into his bullhorn. "Everyone calm down and seek to stop this tomfoolery immediately!"

"What happened here?" Blythe returned from the restroom.

I pointed to the fraying rope attached to the curtain pulley system. "The last bit of rope that's attached to anything other than Chewy is almost gone."

"I've got this." Blythe ripped off her sweater and tied the arms around her neck, creating a makeshift cape. "I'll just tell him to let go."

Side by side, Blythe and Mrs. Darling, stage manager and director, sprinted down the center of the cafetorium.

"Hang on, dear Chewy." Mrs. Darling teared up. "You're a tenacious boy."

From center stage, Janie bellowed, "'You *is* smart! You *is* important!' *The Help*, starring the venerable Viola Davis!"

Chewy swung back over the stage, grabbing at Janie. "Shut up with the movies, and help me!" Chewy screamed, snatching one of the sheets off Janie before swinging back over the audience. As he flew away, the sheet around Janie quickly unraveled, spinning her around, throwing her back to the floor.

The Help had arrived. Quickly, the sheet filled with air like a sail, transforming into a parachute. Chewy looked like a surrendering paratrooper.

"Chewy! You need to let go of the rope!" Blythe directed, the opposite of what Mrs. Darling had said.

"Nooooooooo!" Chewy gripped the rope harder. "I did it all. It was just me. I don't take orders any MOOOOOOOOOORE!"

Cupping my hands, I yelled, "Let go now, Chewy! Surrender!"

Whether he finally listened or his hands just got too tired was anybody's guess, but as he swung toward the back of the cafetorium one last time, he confessed, "I clogged the toilet! I lied! I framed El Pollo Locoooo!" And then giving up completely, he let go of the rope and the sheet just in time to land in Mr. Akins's waiting arms. The principal's face looked like he would be talking to Chewy for a while.

Mrs. Darling ran to Chewy and stroked his hair. "You scared the Dickens out of me."

"Not a scratch on him!" Mr. Akins reported, easing a shaken Chewy to his feet.

"I'm sorry, El," Chewy blathered and cried. "I let the power get to me."

"He's all right, everyone!" Mrs. Darling held up her fist in victory. *"Huzzah!"*

"Hey, Chewy! Teach me that rope trick and we're even," José yelled back from center stage.

The end-of-day bell blasted like an emergency alarm, calling an end to this year's performance of the Actin' Alamos production of *A Christmas Carol*.

Time of death: 3:30 p.m.

Not one clap. Dead silence.

Then the perfect thought hit me. I jumped out onto center stage, almost tripping on the pile of curtains. And I recited the famous ending line, projecting it like I meant it: "God bless us, every one!"

The audience roared with approval, giving us a standing ovation.

And they didn't leave after the bell. They stayed in the cafetorium, clapping, cheering, and wondering how we'd pulled it all off. Nobody wanted it to end.

Maybe they had been thrilled by an amazing feat of acrobatic art. Maybe they were moved by an in-air confession. But one thing was for sure, they loved every minute of our once-in-a-lifetime twist ending of *A Christmas Carol*.

Being number one isn't important. But being part of something *always* is.

"I'm going to be in the next play," Sophia's seventh-grade boyfriend Raymond announced, standing on a chair.

"Yeah," Sophia said, leaping atop the chair next to him. "I want to fly like that bossy yelling boy."

I waved for the cast to join us onstage. We stood there, side by side. Mrs. Darling, the one who brought us together; José, the true Scrooge; Marquis, the one who's not *always* right; Bossy Blythe, the one who's always ready to tell you what to do; Cliché, the one who dropped her role like a hot potato; Janie, the chain-dragging, sheet-styling, movie-quoting ghost; and right next to me, Abhi. We were in the middle of it all.

We joined hands and bowed for the cheering crowd.

Now I know there's really only one role for me to play, and it's the only one I can: Zack Delacruz.

ABOUT THE AUTHOR

JEFF ANDERSON is the author of *Zack Delacruz: Me and My Big Mouth* and *Just My Luck* (*Zack Delacruz: Book 2*). A former teacher, Jeff travels to schools across the country to help students discover the joy and power of writing. Find out more about Jeff at writeguy.net or follow him on Twitter @writeguyjeff. He lives in San Antonio, TX.

ABOUT THE ARTIST

ANDREA MILLER is an illustrator and children's book designer. She lives with her wife, their plant children, and an enormous collection of books in Philadelphia, PA. You can find her work online at blkdiamond.art and talk to her on Twitter @andreacecelia

SIXTH GRADE

Blythe Balboa

Abhijana Bhatt

Janie Bustamante

Zack Delacruz

Janie